THE RIGHT
INTENTION

PRAISE FOR SUCH SMALL HANDS

"Barba inhabits the minds of children with an exactitude that seems to me so uncanny as to be almost sinister."
—*The Guardian*

"Barba is intensely alive to the shifting, even Janus-faced nature of strong feeling." —*San Francisco Chronicle*

"*Such Small Hands* is a magnificently chilling antidote to society's reverence for ideas of infantile innocence and purity."—*Financial Times*

"Barba's stunning and beautiful prose helps us realize that our adult incomprehension is not absolute."—*Los Angeles Review of Books*

"Each one of these pages is exquisite, and the end result is a perfectly expressed work that transmits the perverse and bizarre experience that is youth, where games signify life and death and where relationships are teased and pushed to the breaking point."—*Music & Literature*

"A lyrically rich and devastating portrayal of adolescent struggle."— *ZYZZYVA*

"A darkly evocative work about young girls, grief, and the unsettling, aching need to belong."
—*Kirkus Reviews* (Starred Review)

"Barba explores what the dynamics of an orphanage reveal about any insular community and the trials of its inevitable outcast."—Idra Novey, author of *Ways to Disappear*

THE RIGHT INTENTION

Andrés Barba

Translated from the Spanish by
Lisa Dillman

**TRANSIT
BOOKS**

Published by Transit Books
2301 Telegraph Avenue, Oakland, California 94612
www.transitbooks.org

La recta intención
Copyright © 2002 Andrés Barba
Originally published in Spanish by Editorial Anagrama S.A.
English Translation Copyright © 2018 Lisa Dillman

ISBN: 978-1-945492-06-8
LIBRARY OF CONGRESS CONTROL NUMBER: 2018930165

DESIGN & TYPESETTING
JUSTIN CARDER

DISTRIBUTED BY
CONSORTIUM BOOK SALES & DISTRIBUTION
(800) 283-3572 | CBSD.COM

PRINTED IN THE UNITED STATES OF AMERICA

9 8 7 6 5 4 3 2 1

To the memory of Marcela Martínez,
for the gift that was her life.

To her family: Alberto, Marta, and Felipe,
for teaching me to forgive.

To Jason V. Stone

"I have tormentors then in me, O father?"

"Ay, no few, my son; nay, fearful ones and manifold."

"I do not know them, father."

"Torment the first is this Not–knowing, son."

The Corpus Hermeticum

TABLE OF CONTENTS

The Right Intention

THE RIGHT
INTENTION

NOCTURNE

THE AD IN THE "MALE SEEKING MALE" SECTION SAID:

I'm so alone. Roberto. (91) 4177681.

and was placed among others listing predictable ob-
scenities and a series of oral necessities. Page 43. At the top.
Above a bisexual named Ángel soliciting a threesome and
beneath the photo of a man of indeterminate age and sadness who wore a mask that gave him the pathetic air of a terrorist just emerging from the shower; it said *so alone* just like
that, like it was nothing, it said it with the afternoon languor
pressing in through the living room window (the one that
overlooked the park) almost the way you accept the ritual of
Sunday afternoon boredom, with no resentment.

I'm so alone.

If he had accepted Marta's invitation, he would have an
excuse to get dressed now, go out; the doorman's little desk
would be empty, the street would be empty, the dog would
stare up at him, watery eyes, panting tongue, tail wagging to
the rhythm of his desire to go for a walk, "Platz, paw, sit,"
repeated, the same as the light, an anonymous conversation

beneath his bedroom window, the one that overlooked the courtyard, the cars.

He'd bought it last night and the first thing he did was check the ages of the men who'd placed the ads (almost never stated, which was worse because it meant that the majority of them were probably young). The ones who dared to send a photo took the risk of being recognized. He had gone out to buy cigarettes and ended up buying the magazine. When he got home he started to masturbate to one of the personals but ended up using an erotic art catalogue he'd bought last month. When he finished he washed his hands, made some soup, and fed the dog. There were no movies on TV. Marta called to invite him over for Sunday lunch with Ramón and the kids and he declined, saying he had other plans. But he didn't have other plans. The movies playing at the theater didn't appeal to him enough to make him want to go out, deal with the hassle of the ticket and refreshment lines, and then return home without being able to rave about or even discuss what he'd seen. He hadn't been to an art exhibit in years. He fell asleep thinking tomorrow he would take it easy at home, and it didn't sound like a bad idea. Sometimes he liked to stay in, lose track of time watching TV after lunch, listen to Chopin while lounging on the sofa, leafing through a book. The magazine lay on one of the armchairs like a long and accepted failure. After having used it last night, he thought he'd throw it away, but he'd left it there and when he finished watching the afternoon movie it had sat there, looking up at him saying *Madrid Contactos* on the cover in red letters and *death to hypocrisy* in smaller ones, under the headline and above the photo of a woman who looked like his brother-in-law Ramón's sister because, like her, she wore half a ton of mascara on each eye and her thin lips were made up to look fuller, filled in beyond her lip line. He opened it back up to the "male seeking male" section. He lingered over the pictures again, became excited again.

I'm so alone. Roberto. (91) 4177681.

It dawned on him that this had been going on for many years. Simply, almost painlessly, he had become resigned to the fact that he himself would never demand the things the personals were asking for, and although on a couple of occasions he had contracted a rent boy and brought him up to his apartment, the fact that he had to pay, the whole act of the wallet, the question, the exchange, turned him off to such a degree that he would then become uncomfortable at how long he took and once or twice ended up asking the guy to leave out of sheer disgust.

The dog barked and he found his shoes to take him down for a walk. He left the light on and put on his coat.

Monday everything looked the same from his bank office window. A Coca-Cola sign flashed on and off, as did the recently hung lights announcing the imminent advent of Christmas. He had heard something about an office party and, although he'd said he would go—declining would have launched a desperate search for excuses—they knew, as he did, that it had been years since he last liked Alberto's jokes (always the same, whispered to the new secretary or the newest female graduate hire), Andrés's toasts, and Sandra's conversations about the kids. The fact that he was the oldest employee at the office allowed him to decline those invitations, ignore them without having to worry about subsequent animosities that were felt but never expressed. He enjoyed this in the same way that he enjoyed his solitude, his collection of consolations and little excesses that he had grown used to (Napoleon cognac, fancy cigarettes, a weekly dinner at an expensive restaurant) and which led him to grant that he was a reasonably happy man. Jokes about his homosexuality told in hushed tones at the office met with his indifference, making him invulnerable, and although his exterior coldness had begun as a survival technique, now he really did feel comfortable in it, like someone who has finally found a warm place to take refuge and is content to settle there, without yearning for better.

But the ad in that magazine said:

I'm so alone. Roberto. (91) 4177681.

And those four words, since he read them on Saturday night, had begun to unravel everything. When he finished work on Monday he felt anxious and he didn't know why. Or he did, but didn't want to admit it. Accepting that he wanted to call that number would have meant accepting disorder where, for many long years, there had reigned peace, or something that, without actually being peace, was somehow akin to it: his Napoleon cognac, lunch at Marta's house once every two weeks, walking the dog, the nightly

TV movie he watched until tiredness overcame him, maybe the occasional rent boy he'd bring home in his car and whose presence he would then try to erase as soon as possible, fluffing up the sofa cushions (not the bed, never the bed), opening the windows, repenting.

That night he took the dog for a walk earlier than usual and then it became undeniable. Something had broken. Something fragile and very fine had broken. He always ate dinner first, smoked a cigarette watching TV and then took the dog out. Why hadn't he done that today? The dog hadn't even wagged his tail when he saw him approach with the leash and, on the way down in the elevator, had looked up at him with an expression of bovine wonderment.

"Paw," he said. "Paw," and the dog gave him his paw, tongue out and eyebrows raised, as if his owner were teaching him the rules of a new game.

When he got back he looked for the magazine. He'd left it on the table, he was sure, and now it wasn't there. He looked in the bathroom, and in the kitchen. He shuffled through his desk drawers. Any other day at this time he would have already had dinner and be smoking his cigarette, getting ready to walk the dog, yet that night not only had he not done it but he was also nervous, desperately searching for that magazine that he wouldn't even have been able to masturbate to without the help of the erotic art catalogue he'd bought last month. Finding himself in this situation increased his desperation, but he didn't give up until he found it. It was on the floor beside the sofa. He opened it again, and became excited reading the personals again, but there was something a little different. It wasn't the TV, or the cognac, or the dog, but himself, in the midst of all those other things. Reading all of the ads was a game he submitted to, fooling himself and yet all the while knowing precisely what he was looking for. Page 43. At the top. Above a bisexual named Ángel soliciting a threesome and beneath the photo of the nude man with the mask.

I'm so alone. Roberto. (91) 4177681.

Finding it was like feigning surprise when an expected visitor arrives, except this time the surprise was real; it was as if the ad had never been there and he had invented it at the bank. He had never met anyone named Roberto, so—though it was a common name—it hovered there on page 43 like a riddle waiting to be solved. It wasn't an ugly name. Roberto. Anxiety made him eat the steaks he was saving for the weekend. Now he'd have to go shopping again because the leftover rice he'd been planning to have tonight would go bad by tomorrow. This was no good at all. Not that it was bad to have eaten something he was saving for another time; that was the sort of luxury that made him reasonably happy. But doing it the way he'd done it, just like that, for no reason. But really, had there been reasons the other times?

Half an hour later he couldn't sleep. He always went to bed early, capitalizing on television's soporific effect, and that night he couldn't sleep. He'd taken the magazine with him to bed and left it on his nightstand. He picked it up and opened it but then felt ridiculous. It was all Roberto's fault.

In the open wardrobe door, he could see the dark, faint reflection of his fifty-six-year-old body in the glow of the television, projecting tiredness and an obesity that, while not obscene, he had never made a serious attempt to combat. He felt pathetic for having entered into the game Roberto was proposing. How—after so many years of reasonable happiness, of peace—could so blatant a ploy have gotten the better of him? Crumpling it up, he took it to the kitchen and threw it in the trash. Then he tied the bag and left it by the door, hoping that the doorman would not have made his rounds yet. Sleep descended upon him that night serene and unburdened. He was proud of himself.

In the morning the trash bag was gone. He could have verified this simply by looking out the peephole but instead he opened the door. At the bank, they asked him if he felt all right when he arrived.

"I have a little bit of a headache," he said.

"It's the flu. People are dropping like flies."

But it wasn't the flu. The Coca-Cola sign flashed on and off, as did the Christmas lights. It was Christmastime. How had he not realized? Two years ago he'd felt a slow-burning sadness during the holidays, too, and he hadn't been able to shake it off until they had taken the lights down. But what he felt now wasn't really sadness. He was anxious. He made a mistake keying in the number of a bank account and spent almost half an hour arguing with a customer who claimed his deposits were not being credited correctly. At lunchtime he went to get the first-aid kit to take his temperature. But he had no fever. He took an aspirin. But he didn't have a headache. The ad said:

I'm so alone. Roberto, and then there was a phone number. He couldn't remember the number. He, who had always been so proud of his numeric memory, couldn't recall the number. It started 417. It started 417 and then there was something like 4680. It wasn't 4680 but it was similar to 4680. 5690. 3680. *(91) 4177681*

I'm so alone. Roberto, and then 417. . .

When he left the bank he didn't go home but instead walked to the kiosk where he'd bought the personals magazine the other day.

"Check over there," the newsagent said.

It wasn't there.

"Don't you have any more?"

"Aren't there any there?"

"I can't see any."

"Then we must be out."

He couldn't find it at the sex shop three blocks down, either, and the clerk hadn't even heard of the magazine. He thought about filing a complaint but that seemed ridiculous. When he got home the dog was restless because he'd been gone so long. He was hungry and wagged his tail. Any other day he'd have felt relaxed arriving home, but this time he didn't know what to do, he didn't know if he should sit down or watch TV. He hadn't eaten dinner yet. He had to walk the dog. Suddenly every act that, for years, he had performed in a ritual of leisurely contentment seemed an unbearable obligation. He put on the dog's leash and went down to take him for a walk but didn't follow his usual route. When he got back, though he had no appetite, he ate dinner and then took two sleeping pills. He dreamed of someone he had loved for three long years, ages ago, but couldn't see his face; there was only the familiar presence of that body lying beside him, his smell, his saliva.

Tuesday and Wednesday and Thursday he went to the bank with a fever. He felt weak but at the same time he wanted to scream. It seemed impossible to him that he had held on this way for so many years. During his lunch break he went out to his usual café-bar for a sandwich and coffee but he felt excluded from everything around him. Wherever he looked, all he saw were couples, kisses, little signs of affection. The cold condescension he once looked on with now turned against him, blowing up in his face with envy and anxiety. He had to find that magazine. Now.

I'm so alone, said Roberto. He was alone, too. He wanted to be kissing someone, like all those couples, holding someone's hand, buying presents. He could waste no more time on irony.

It was all so easy. He didn't have to walk more than a block, as he'd expected. He went up to the first newsstand he saw and said "Madrid Contactos" and the newsagent held out a copy of the magazine.

"Three hundred fifty pesetas."

The elation almost made him mock the scandalized expression an old woman buying the newspaper gave him; there was the woman who looked like his brother-in-law Ramón's sister, arms crossed to push out her breasts, thin lips made up beyond the lip line like a quick fix for the standard displeasure caused by her body, and there, too, would be, on page 43, at the top, Roberto, above that bisexual named Ángel and beneath the photo of the man with the mask on. He asked for a bag, slipped the magazine in it and walked towards the bank almost in a good mood, but another fear was born in the remaining hours of his workday. What was he going to do now? Was he really planning to call that number? And if he wasn't planning to call, then why had he gone through all that? He took a taxi home. He went up to his apartment without greeting the doorman and as soon as he closed the door he turned to page 43.

(91) 4177681.

How could he have forgotten such an easy number? But that wasn't the problem.

The dog looked at him with eyes watering at his forgotten walk, and he said, "Paw."

The animal held out a weary paw, like the child asked for the umpteenth time to repeat a once-funny remark, and he decided he would think the matter over on the walk. But there was nothing to think about. Roberto's phone number began to pound in his head as soon as he got outside; it was now as clear and easy to remember as the jingle from a commercial *(91) 4177681*, he'd call just to hear what his voice sounded like, that was all, he'd call and then hang up, he'd have a nice tumbler of cognac, watch a movie, yes, there was a good one on that night, he had seen it listed in the paper, it wouldn't be hard to fall asleep.

He waited until ten-thirty to do it. Ten o'clock seemed too early and he never called anyone after eleven. Ten-thirty was a good time. It rang three times before anyone answered.

"Yes?" Roberto's voice said.

The voice sounded young, younger than he'd imagined after reading the ad. It was easy to imagine a small apartment, maybe roommates, a narrow hallway, clothes strewn over the bed, the TV in the background, a cheap dinner.

"Hello?"

He thought about someone he had loved once, for three long years, ages ago. He didn't know why, but that voice had something of the shy, impressionable boy he himself had been when that someone loved him. Roberto hung up, and he thought, as he listened to the intermittent dial tone, about the night when that someone had put flowers in his hair, lipstick on his lips, taken a shower with him. He couldn't remember his face, but his presence was there. He remembered his hands, his tongue, the messy apartment, the strange feeling of having possessed each other that filled their conversations with an easy tranquility, with jokes, with silence, the world waking up blue and acceptable, the word happiness, the word love, on his lips with a naturalness that had seemed simple and universal.

It started to rain, as if even the sky were trying to make his crime more obvious, and he dialed the number again.

"Yes?"

"Hello, I was calling because . . . I read your ad."

"Did you call a minute ago?"

"Yes."

"Why didn't you say anything?"

"I was afraid."

He woke up that morning and went into the living room. There was the glass that Roberto had drunk from, the butts of the cigarettes he had smoked, the indentation his weight had left on the sofa. He smiled, recalling how enthusiastically he had tasted that fine, old cognac that was reserved for special occasions, his shock at learning how much a bottle of it cost.

"That's more than I earn in four days," Roberto said, looking through the glass at the ochre liquid, and he sniffed it again, and tasted it again, barely moistening his lips, and smiled again with that mixture of nervousness and strange happiness that shone in his eyes all night.

While they were on the phone, after his admission of fear, Roberto had asked him how old he was and he had said fifty. He could pass for fifty. People always said he didn't look his age.

"I'm twenty-one," Roberto had said, almost apologetic.

The silence that followed almost made him hang up because he assumed Roberto was disappointed by his age, that he was looking for a younger man, that it wouldn't be long before he found an excuse to reject him. But Roberto didn't reject him.

"Do you still want to meet up?"

"Of course," he replied. "But . . . now?"

"Why not?"

They met in a plaza that Roberto said was close to his house. He drove there before the appointed time and waited in the car, with the lights out. He saw the boy arrive, light a cigarette, button the top button of his jacket when it started to rain again, take refuge under one of the plaza's arcades. His slenderness, the straight hair falling over his ears, held a strange beauty. He wasn't handsome, but he was definitely attractive and he thought that he would like to dress like that, like Roberto, and to be twenty and to walk up from behind and scare him, walk down the street holding hands with him. The few people who were still out at that time of night had something in common in their coats, their shoes, the color of their eyes. He was the only one who seemed different. By the way he was dressed one might have guessed he was homeless, and yet he thought he looked like the whole world belonged to him: the street, the cars, even the people passing by. He got out of the car and walked towards him. Roberto had been staring at him since he closed the car door.

"Hi," he said, with something approaching a smile.

"Hi. Disappointed?" he asked.

"No. Are you?"

"No."

On the way back to the apartment Roberto stared at him from the passenger's seat, grinning the whole way. Their excitement was contagious, and neither of them could sit still. Roberto rolled down the window and he did the same. He felt the fresh air on his face, like a lovely awakening. What would come next? What was it about that street, within it, that gave it a strange, different life, one that went beyond just being there, leading somewhere? The night filled with trees when they held hands after getting out of the car, and when they rode up in the elevator, and when they walked into the apartment.

"I love your house," said Roberto.

"Thank you."

Roberto seemed encouraged by his good mood and laughter, which was actually just a nervous reaction. What was he supposed to do now? Kiss him? Offer him a drink? While he was getting the cognac, Roberto told him that he worked in a Laundromat during the day and then at a bar until ten. The money wasn't great, but it was enough to rent his own apartment. He handed him the cognac, sat down beside him on the sofa and stroked his hair. Roberto looked down, picked up his glass, and moistened his lips. He was so seduced by that artless discomfort that he waited patiently for Roberto to look up at him again as he stroked his hair, tucking it back behind his ears. When he did, Roberto's eyes were riveted and serious, concentrated on not missing a single movement of his pupils. He leaned in towards him slowly. They kissed. Roberto's lips were thin and tasted vaguely of cognac. He closed his eyes and put a hand on his back, simulating an embrace he didn't quite dare to carry out. He couldn't recall ever having kissed anyone so carefully. When he looked at him again, the boy raised his eyes once more, smiling. The hand that had been on his back now reached for the glass, brought it to his lips. Roberto took it out of his hand and set it on the table and kissed him again. His lips were half-parted, his tongue ventured tentatively, and he held him and stroked his hair as he let himself be kissed. He thought the next step was logical: he reached for Roberto's zipper to undo it and noted the boy's excitement as he did. Immediately, Roberto stopped him.

"Not so soon . . . We just met. Remember?"

He didn't know what to say.

"If we do it tonight I'm going to feel very bad about myself in the morning. You don't want me to feel bad about myself, do you?"

The question had a childish, almost virginal, tone.

"No."

"I'm sure you understand."

"Of course I do, that's fine, I'm sorry," he said, pulling away a little.

"Once I did it with a guy the first night and he never called me again."

That twenty-one-year-old boy's body, without having been seen, took on a more powerful intensity and what had seemed a ridiculous, juvenile modesty less than five minutes ago suddenly squared in his mind with mathematical clarity and precision; the wait was essential, and pleasant, and just.

"I like the way you touch me, though."

Roberto curled up in his arms, tucking his feet beneath him on the sofa, and leaned on his shoulder. His hair was still wet from the rain; his thinness, his little nose, the arm around his waist gave him the appearance of a wet, shivering cat. He felt surprisingly justified in protecting him.

The Coca-Cola sign flashed on and off, as did the Christmas lights, but at twelve o'clock that night, when he headed towards his usual bar, the light lent the memory of Roberto the unreal quality typical of all things nocturnal. Nevertheless, when he had gotten up that morning, the glass Roberto had drunk from was still on the table, next to a pack of cigarettes he had left behind and a lighter that said Laundromat; the imprint of his body on the cushions had not yet been erased.

They saw each other again that night, and the next, and the next. The third time Roberto came over, he gave him a copy of his apartment key. They just sat and talked about anything. He had bought some modern music that he thought Roberto might like and he put it on when the boy arrived, pretending that it was what he listened to all the time.

"You don't like this music," Roberto said, after three songs.

"How do you know?"

"It's written all over your face."

"But don't you like it?"

"I do, yeah, but there's no reason you have to like everything I like."

Without saying anything, he felt ashamed at some of their recent conversations. The fear of upsetting Roberto had led him to feign enthusiasm for childish things a couple of times and when he did, he had feared that Roberto would be able to tell.

"Put on the music you listen to when you're alone," Roberto proposed.

"When I'm alone I listen to Chopin."

"Then put that on."

The nocturnes flowed through the house like an exquisite lie over dinner.

"Isn't it beautiful?"

"Very. I've never listened to Chopin. What is this called?"

"These are the nocturnes."

It wasn't hard to impress Roberto, talking about the bank and the stock market, but he soon stopped doing it because he feared the admiration would turn into some sort of perpetual self-praise. What he most loved about those nights was the way they yielded to silence, the way he would come up and kiss him in the middle of a conversation, his silent, slender, almost domestic character, walking to the bathroom or coming back from the kitchen after going to get another beer. He lacked initiative when it came to love games and yet, he would always win by loving whoever loved him. All of Roberto's affective sensibilities lay dormant and depended upon his own activity, so when he lightly touched his hand or chin or hair, he had the impression that some instinctual jolt forced him to return twice the kisses and cuddles received. It wasn't a nervous thing, but a visceral need to be appreciated. If a lull came over the conversation, Roberto would come up to him and rest a head on his shoulder and play with his fingers. That wasn't nerves, either, just an exploratory kind of tenderness, a means of sounding things out, trying to find the right way. His life, like the lives of compassionate, empathetic people, took the joys and pains of others and made them his own: he felt everything.

"Last night I dreamed you didn't want to see me anymore, that I came over and your house was full of people and you acted like you didn't even know me."

He realized, on those evenings, that what made Roberto have those nightmares wasn't very different from what made him not want to let the boy go home at night. The speed with which it had all come about, the strange way that they had met, left them naked in a space that had to be invented, one whose laws were the fruit not of delibera-tion—which did not exist—or normal patterns of behavior, but pure conduct; stroking Roberto's hair, holding his hand, kissing him, these were not things he did out of convention, or even desire—even if desire was what drove them most urgently—it was the anxiousness to create a habitable space, a hermetic language that couldn't be understood by anyone else. That feeling, together with Roberto's habitual silence, tinged those afternoons with a solemn languor.

The fourth night he came over they hardly talked. Roberto sat down beside him without even taking off his coat, undid the button and zipper of his pants and started to stroke him. He didn't say anything. Roberto moved slowly, looking into his eyes the whole time. He thought there was something deeply sad in the figure of that boy who he was growing to love, like a strange and distant part of himself, and he was afraid he would stop loving him, but he was also afraid that he would stop being loved by him. He caressed Roberto's cheek and the boy closed his eyes but did not stop masturbating him. Behind his eyelids there must have shone the pleasure of someone who has consciously decided to do something just to make someone else happy. When Roberto had finished, he reciprocated, except that the boy became somewhat tense once he got his belt unbuckled.

"Do you want me to?"

"Yes."

He convulsed a couple of times and his stomach contracted almost imperceptibly and he came quickly, with almost no stimulation. Then the boy buried his face in his shoulder and it suddenly felt wet.

"Are you crying?"

He tilted his head up, placing a finger under his chin so he could look at him straight on.

"Why are you crying?"

"I don't know," he answered, clasping onto his neck, still shaking, like a happy child, impenetrable.

He liked hearing stories about Roberto's life and when he could tell he was getting ready to tell one (crossing his legs on the sofa, taking a sip from his glass, fanning out his fingers in an explanatory gesture), he felt the pleasure of someone ready to be seduced by a tale normally no more eventful than falling off a bicycle, or an episode of comic embarrassment, or some family anecdote that was made up, the way all family anecdotes are made up. After a week he realized, in shock, that except for having feigned juvenile enthusiasm a couple of times, he had not told a single lie, and if he hadn't told any lies it was because the whole thing seemed like a lie; from Roberto's hands to the way his hair fell, from his pants to his recollections of his mother; a lie that the walls of the apartment, the enclosure, made possible.

"I love your house," Roberto had said the first time he'd walked in the door.

The keepsakes had accumulated within those four walls like a chorus line on a stage, and what at first had been no more than a shabby, unfurnished house had slowly evolved, since he'd bought it twenty years ago, into something functional, and then comfortable. But now, for the first time, he didn't just feel comfortable among his things, he felt proud of them, because Roberto had admired them. That's why part of the game of the first few evenings together had been Roberto asking him about where everything around him had come from. The carefulness with which he approached each object, with which he stroked it when he picked it up and asked "What about this one?" was part of the ritual that, from the start, they had both understood was vital. Roberto was naming the elements of paradise, giving them features and contours, and the boy was happy in his role as Adam, whereas he, whom this twenty-one-year-old had slowly yet ceaselessly begun to hurt, understood that after the euphoria of discovery Roberto would soon realize that their Eden, like all Edens, was a cloistered place, and that what now seemed dazzling would end up stifling him.

Those nights he dreamed repeatedly of lakes and huge expanses of grass where naked boys lay kissing each other in slow motion. They were silent dreams, leisurely dreams, and all the boys in them did was touch each other and laugh. There was something definitively tender and simple about them, old although they were young, and he recalled himself in the dream taking shelter behind the reeds. It seemed strange to him to note that he, whose erotic imagery in fantasies tended to be violent, woke up content and to recall that in the dream he had not even approached the boys, but had been happy just to watch them.

Whenever Roberto went home, things would take another tack. While it seemed reasonable that someone like him would lose his head over a twenty-one-year-old boy, the inverse struck him as perverse. To love an old man like him (though he wasn't an old man yet, not really), to love an old man the way Roberto loved him, you had to either be lying or wicked. Maybe Roberto was lying, maybe he was just trying to get money out of him (but what money?), maybe it was just morbid curiosity, maybe he was laughing at him right now (why would he do that?), in front of a group of boys his age; that was the most natural explanation, the most reasonable explanation (but what did those words mean? *natural, reasonable*). Maybe he was saying, "The old man is all alone, he's sad. It's pitiful," (but why would he say that?) maybe he was already over him and that's why he was so silent, or maybe he was just stupid (but Roberto wasn't stupid), or he was lying (but someone who lies wouldn't have written that personal ad) or he was lonely.

The sound of his steps when he arrived, the bell in the elevator, wiping his shoes on the mat—he was waiting on the sofa, that's why he could always hear him—and then the sound of the key in the door, jangling against other keys for other doors that he didn't know, that maybe he'd never know, and then his breathless, smiling figure walking in.

"You have no idea how cold it is out there."

And again, searching the depths of his fear, waiting for the boy to approach when he didn't want to wait but to run to him and kiss him, like some newly married shop girl, and Roberto taking off his coat and tossing it onto the sofa and coming up to him, smiling, "I'm serious, you have no idea how cold it is," Roberto's moist lips, his hair, his cheeks slightly flushed from the heating.

"What? You don't believe me? Feel my hands, they're freezing."

That boy who he would no longer be able to surprise, because in barely a week he'd already gotten over his astonished admiration of the house, the stories about the bank, the cognac.

They decided to watch a video that night. He had rented it that afternoon and Roberto admitted, when he saw the cover, that he'd never even heard of it. He would never remember the title but he remembered that the story was about a fourteen-year-old boy who is traumatized by the death of his father. The boy oscillates between pain and cynicism; the accident that ended his father's life suddenly had shaken him so badly, brought him to the very limits of what a person could endure, that it had provoked a different self, one that looked on the suffering of others, and even his own suffering, with a Mephistophelic irony. So at the funeral, when he saw his mother cry and flail her arms around grotesquely, the boy thought with a coldness that distressed even himself, "Good acting, Mother, that would be great on stage."

He recognized a little of himself in the movie. He, too, had made fun of others' pain, and of his own, with that sort of coldness, and if he'd done it, it was because most of the time he couldn't find any compelling reason to love the peo-

ple who surrounded him. Any show of love he considered
an act of voluntary blindness that, when undertaken, was
done only out of a physical need for protection, or affection,
and always with the expectation that it would be returned,
if not immediately, then in the near future. With Roberto
it was different. While others were judged and sentenced
almost a priori, Roberto walked on water. Others tried to
save themselves, to be accepted, to appear pleasant. Roberto was silent, naked, complete. How could he be cynical
about him?

When he turned to look at him he saw that he had been
hugging his knees since he turned off the television.

"Roberto."

"What?"

"Did you like the movie?"

"No."

"Why not?"

"I don't know."

"What are you thinking?"

"I'm thinking that the world is ugly and people are all
unhappy."

He leaned over to kiss him.

"Even me?"

"No, not you."

"Do you want to stay over tonight?"

"Yes."

They went into the bedroom. Roberto sat down on the
bed to take off his shoes and socks.

"Stand up," he said, and Roberto obeyed quickly, smiling. He unbuttoned his shirt, slowly. He helped him off with his undershirt. Every action produced an immediate and identical reaction in Roberto, and although he liked that, for the first time he thought that the boy's love could never reach beyond the walls of his apartment, that everything that was tender there would be ridiculous or dirty or perverted outside. Soon they were both naked and Roberto jumped under the covers quickly, laughing at having escaped his embrace. He was happy. Radiant. He looked out at him, the covers pulled up to his nose, and his eyes gave away his big, open smile. He gave in to the game of chase eagerly, forgetting his doubts without much trouble.

Holding Roberto's naked body filled him with a sense of emptiness. He'd had similar experiences years ago, but those had been unpleasant and this filled him with a curious placidness. He had never encountered a body that was as aware of its nakedness as Roberto's and yet, at the same time, displayed itself so gaily. Nudity was therefore not what it normally was: a presence that was exhausted as it displayed itself, where the mind was able to progress not towards awareness but towards a void that expanded in free fall toward a world in which Roberto was the only teacher, one of pure and simple perception. He must have been exhausted because he fell asleep right away, one arm around the pillow and the other around his waist. He envied the immediacy with which Roberto's youth allowed him to get what he wanted and recalled the years when he, too, had only to close his eyes in order to fall asleep. He moved Roberto's hand and turned on the bedside light. He turned around to see if Roberto had woken up, but he'd barely fluttered his eyelids. His pupils appeared and disappeared in the whites of his eyes like a spoon dipping into a glass of milk. In the room's silence he could hear his breathing, slow and tired. The world howled at the windows in gusts of wind.

But the sadness remained. The week and a half of his relationship with Roberto had momentarily hidden but not resolved, it. The most basic uncertainties surged in the most basic, most straightforward ways, into the bedroom, the living room, the bathroom whenever he was alone. What could he do now? Thinking about the future was like poking his head into a dark hole from which he could feel the panting breath of some beast. It was as if he were afraid to live, as if he'd forgotten all of the coping mechanisms, the tricks, the lies that made life habitable. How could he possibly show anyone the love he felt for that boy if he himself didn't believe it entirely? If Roberto called to say he was going to be a little late, he'd start to panic, thinking he didn't really want to see him, or that he'd met someone else, and that thought, as ridiculous as it might have been, as ridiculous as even he realized that it was, started a downward spiral, made him uneasy and at the same time unable to do anything but picture him somewhere else, with someone else, laughing.

Then Roberto would arrive and he could breathe again, he'd feel himself taking the reins little by little, getting hold of the situation. The simple presence of that silent individual would calm his fears once again.

"Did you think about me today?"

"I thought about you lots."

"Really?"

"You were everywhere."

The silence that formed the normal rhythm of those evenings allowed him to take his place in the world and, simultaneously, to watch Roberto. One of those nights it occurred to him that he would never know the boy any better than he did already. All that was left from then on was to learn his likes and dislikes, his reactions, the way he smiled, the way he half-closed his eyes and, although that was the usual way of getting to know someone, in Roberto those were no more than details that gave a little more definition to his initial impression, which was correct, and just. So on those nights, the coquetry he had intuited spontaneously at first materialized in a colored nail polish collection Roberto used to paint his toenails carefully while he looked on in silence, finding a simple solution to life yet again, lacking difficulties beyond those disdained for being all-embracing or infinitesimal. And what was wrong with that? He needed the presence of that twenty-one-year-old, his dark hair falling over his ears, his uncertain smile—part pained, part open— he needed the love and the secrets of that strange creature named Roberto to escape the feeling that life was going to fall apart at every turn.

On Christmas Day he went to Marta's house for dinner in a good mood. Ramón had made sea bass and the meal was pleasant, though the children made a racket the entire time. Marta said she thought he was looking very well, and Ramón's sister, who had also come for dinner that night—and who every year rather than looking more exhausted or frumpier wore more make-up—concurred. He was delighted by everything. Even Ramón's jokes. Something was different, and he didn't realize what it was until the evening was almost over. He had always sat at that table feeling distant from Marta. She, at least, had Ramón. But the closest things he could remember feeling were that summer in Florence, a well in a cortile in Pisa, beside a fountain, a naked boy who looked at him on a beach in Geneva, the smell of oysters in a restaurant while feeling a hand on his thigh, his face in the mirror wearing lipstick, but these were not memories of a specific person, an individual who he missed; rather, they were like passages from a novel you could never return to, a novel whose pages are remembered, reconstructed, inevitably embellished, and, therefore, feel distinctly fictional. After that, the identical years at the bank, repeated in his memory as if they were one long day of routines and predetermined movements, and now Roberto. What to do. What to say. And why.

* * *

It broke the same way as fragile glass, as a thread holding on to a button. He was at home waiting for Roberto to arrive the day after Christmas and the phone rang. It wasn't Marta, it was José Luis from the bank. Informing him that he had to go to Barcelona. Three years ago, copying the American-style business plan, the group his bank belonged to had begun the practice of sending an experienced employee to every new city where they opened a branch, to hold meetings and talk about his or her experiences. He had taken those trips frequently, even requested them. He'd always liked leaving Madrid for a few days and living someplace else, with his travel expenses and hotel paid for. But now there was Roberto. He couldn't leave now.

"I can't," he said.

"I'm not asking you if you can; I'm telling you that you will."

And he felt, on hearing that, that something was breaking. He took leaving Madrid as an imposed abandonment. He would go, and when he returned, nothing would be the same. Roberto would have changed, he wouldn't love him anymore (but why wouldn't he?), he'd say he'd met someone else while he was away, or he'd just gotten bored, young people got bored easily, they changed boyfriends all the time.

He was almost afraid to tell Roberto when he arrived, but he loved the idea.

"You're so lucky," he said.

"So you don't mind if I go?"

"Of course not. Why would I mind?"

They talked about their respective Christmas dinners. Roberto's had been predictable, keeping in mind what little he knew about the family he hardly ever spoke of. Both of his sisters had brought their husbands to dinner and one of them announced what her dress had made obvious a month ago: she was pregnant. Roberto said he was excited to be an uncle. But this was not the conversation he wanted to be having.

"Are you sure you want me to go to Barcelona?"

"Of course."

That's what Roberto's replies were always like, enthusiastic and direct, like blows.

"Hey, what are you doing?"

"I want to paint your toenails."

"Oh no, none of that."

"Come on, please."

He gave in quickly and Roberto got out all his little colored bottles. He stroked the boy's hair while he was lining them up on the table.

"How long will you be there for?"

"Five days."

"So you'll be back for New Year's Eve."

"Why do you ask?"

"No reason. It's just there's a party we could go to."

"Can't we stay here that night?"

"What for?"

"To be together. I don't want to go to a party. We can make dinner here. Have a little champagne. Take a shower . . ."

"But I want to go to this party. We can do those other things any night."

"I know."

Suddenly, Roberto was twenty-one. Why wouldn't a twenty-one-year-old boy want to go to a New Year's Eve party? If he sometimes forgot how old he was, it was because he seemed older, because he half-closed his eyes like an adult, he was quiet like an adult, and he listened. But he was twenty-one. It had become clear, again, and when it became clear he felt as if he was corrupting him, as if the reason he was so afraid to let anyone else know about their relationship was because he himself was embarrassed of it. But he wasn't embarrassed, he was just scared. Afraid he would stop loving him, or stop being loved by him. Roberto was leaning over his feet. His bangs fell over his eyes and his lips were contorted, like someone concentrating so hard on a task they look ridiculous without realizing it. He looked ugly now. Now he was just a kid who worked in a bar and a Laundromat, who didn't understand anything, because Roberto did not understand him, how could a twenty-one-year-old boy understand him? He tried to remember what he had been like at that age but all he could muster up was a few fleeting images of Marta, of a boy he had liked at university and who he'd gone out drinking beer with on occasion, of his mother. Roberto had put on the Chopin record. Ever since he'd said that was what he liked, that was what Roberto put on. And now he was getting tired of Chopin, and he was getting tired of Roberto's expression, his stubbornness over this stupid party, and even the fact that he hadn't been upset about his trip to Barcelona. Because, really, didn't his lack of concern about the trip imply some degree of indifference? If he didn't care about the trip to Barcelona, it meant that deep down the boy was not as interested in him as he'd thought.

"All done. You like it?"

His toenails twinkled up at him, yellow, and blue, and red.

"Now you have to blow on them, like this, so they dry."

Roberto smiled as he blew, and suddenly he felt a little fit of rage. But it wasn't rage, it was pain. No, it wasn't pain, either. He raised the boy's head and kissed him violently. Roberto, though at first he played along, was a little confused by that reaction. He began to undress him, quickly, and after the initial doubt, Roberto seemed happy to join in the game and do it right there on the sofa, for no apparent reason. It was different. There was absolutely no doubt now. He pulled down his pants and went down on him. But not the way he usually did, not slowly, not feeling like he saw himself reflected in the boy the way on other nights he'd thought he saw himself reflected in the boy. He was, simply, sucking Roberto's dick, and realizing this made him feel comfortable momentarily because he knew all about that. Sex was simple, what tortured him was what was beneath the sex; that was why he felt comfortable. Sucking Roberto's dick was a simple act with no consequences as long as it stopped there. It was the rest of it that made him suffer, the other things: the same Chopin melody, the life Roberto led that he knew nothing of. Roberto would leave him, he was sure, sooner or later, he would get bored, he'd turn up one day and invent some absurd excuse to leave him, and he would have to go back to the bank as if it were no big deal, as if nothing had happened, as if nothing had ever happened. That's why it was better this way, treating him like a blow-up doll.

He was so lost in these thoughts that he didn't even realize that Roberto had stopped playing along. The boy had stopped touching him some time ago, and when he realized he was slowing down, too, he lifted his head. He was kneeling in front of Roberto, who looked down on him with something like compassion from what seemed an impossible height.

"What's wrong?" he asked.

There was no recriminating tone in his voice, just pity, just something that, like pity was slow and difficult.

"Can't you see I'm an old man?"

"Come on, you're not an old man, you're only fifty."

"I'm fifty-six."

There was a long silence, as if those six years, and not the lie, had opened a wound that would never heal, as if fifty-six was, really, the maximum expression of old age.

"In twenty years," he went on, "when you are a gorgeous forty-year-old man, a healthy, mature man, I'll need help eating and getting dressed because it will be too hard for me to do on my own anymore. Did you ever think of that?"

"No."

"Well, it's true."

"I'll help you eat and get dressed," Roberto replied, after a short silence, and he couldn't help but smile.

"Don't do that, don't smile like that. Don't make me feel bad."

"I don't want you to feel bad, I just want to tell you what will happen in the end."

"But you love me, right?"

"Of course."

The trip to Barcelona was one long replay of that conversation. Why had he said "of course" when Roberto asked him if he loved him? Why hadn't he just said "yes" or "I love you"? His unhappiness at having to be away from Roberto was compounded by the tediousness of the meetings. He hardly left the hotel out of fear that Roberto might call and he wouldn't be able to answer the phone right away. If Roberto didn't call him in the late afternoon from the bar, then he called him at night. Roberto thought the perfect conversation was one in which he said he loved him and missed him to death, over and over and over. He often asked him what he was wearing. Roberto would kiss the telephone mouthpiece.

"Last night I dreamed that you were here, with me,

and we didn't have to go anywhere and I was painting your nails."

"They're still painted."

"I know."

It's not that he didn't actually miss him, but he realized that he missed him in a different way. Ever since he'd confessed his real age, ever since Roberto's surprise, since the "I love you" question, he had sometimes felt that the end of their relationship was imminent, and that seemed logical, almost acceptable, but other times, especially at night, the world once again became a complex machine in which it would be impossible to live without the boy's help.

The third night, the phone woke him in the middle of the night. It was Roberto. He was calling from a phone booth. His voice was choked and it seemed he was trying not to cry. A group of boys had been waiting for him when he left the bar. He knew one of them by sight. When he walked out they spat at him and called him faggot. He tried to keep moving, but the episode went on for some time, for as long as it had taken him to get to a busy street. The boys had run off when they saw the police car and Roberto stood there, motionless and pathetic like a tree with no leaves. He took off his jacket and wiped the spit from his face and hair. He, who was not violent, recounted this story violently, rabidly, in order to survive.

"They didn't hurt you, did they?"

"No. I would have preferred that. They wanted to humiliate me and they did."

"No, no they didn't."

There was a long silence in which he heard a bus accelerate, and the sound of a car horn.

"Bastards," said something that sounded like Roberto's voice.

"I wish I were there so I could hug you."

"I wish you were here so you could hug me, too."

"Roberto."

"What?"

"I love you."

He'd said it without thinking, it was a logical procession, a necessary one, but as soon as he said it he felt afraid. Roberto didn't answer and his silence made the solemnity palpable. His eyes passed over the objects in the room: the towels on the sofa, the television, the mini-bar, the night pushing in through the windows.

"Really?"

"Yes."

Again the towels, the television, again the fear.

"I love you, too."

The day after that, which was the last day of his trip, they did not repeat those words although they spoke on the phone. Roberto's silence at the end of the conversation awaited their repetition without too much insistence although it was enough to make his need for them palpable. And he, in turn, felt as if those words, the recollection of those words, had suddenly drilled a hole in the wall that would now be impossible to repair, and if he felt frightened when he landed back in Madrid, it was because he realized that now there was no longer any doubt, he was vulnerable.

Roberto was waiting for him at the apartment. He had asked for the day off in order to surprise him, and assured him that it had not been easy, because it was December 31 and they were having a party at the bar where he worked. When he hugged him he felt Roberto's body with a sense of novelty, his arms, his hair. He tasted like cigarettes and mint-flavored gum and he looked different, too, more filled out somehow.

"You look gorgeous."

"Thank you."

He had brushed his hair and was wearing a new shirt, ironed, and nice shoes.

"I wanted to look good when you got back."

Roberto really was splendid in his beauty that afternoon. They talked about everything except the unpleasant incident with the gang of boys and every time he brought up something amusing he felt caught up in the boy's laugh, felt a part of it, and at the same time contemplated how much of his own life had also been lived by Roberto, from afar. The boy remembered every tiny detail of the collection of anecdotes he'd told about his meetings, the names of all the people, the jokes that had been told, as if he had been there.

They made love slowly that night and drank cognac naked on the unmade bed. His body smelled of sweat and cologne. He noticed that Roberto had cleaned the apartment and left a bunch of daisies by the mirror and sunflowers in the bathroom.

"Where did you get the flowers?"

"Well, it's about time! I thought you were never going to notice!" A smile of contained indignation broke out. "I bought them at the market yesterday. I love daisies and sunflowers . . . Have you ever seen Van Gogh's sunflowers? They're so beautiful."

Again, the child. Roberto had brought Van Gogh to him, right there on the sheets, was windmilling his arms in the air to imitate the starry night. It wasn't that he didn't like Van Gogh, but he felt a sort of indulgent affection for him, like a childish passion, crude and impressionable. And there was Roberto, lost in praise for his strong colors and passionate brushstrokes, of course, drifting away from him again. How could he introduce this child to anyone? What was he thinking? He let the predictable conversation about cut-off ears and hysteria run its course, and when it died down, Roberto became the boy he'd dreamed about for five long days once more. He envied his youth again, his agility when he watched him leap out of bed to run naked to the bathroom. He had been that way once, too.

"Well, we have to get dressed soon," he said when he came back, pausing in the bedroom doorway.

"Get dressed for what?"

"For the party. Don't you remember the party I told you about tonight?"

"I don't want to go to any party, I want to stay here with you."

"But don't you remember? We talked about it. And besides, I already bought you a ticket."

"Well. I can just picture what it will be like, this party."

He didn't want to go, so everything Roberto said about the venue, the friends who would be there, the open bar, seemed to confirm his decision not to go rather than entice him. What would he do surrounded by all those boys? Wouldn't he seem ridiculous? Wouldn't they laugh at him? He'd always felt an almost visceral disdain for those people who held on to some absurd sense of adolescence when they were too old to do so, who refused to dress their age, who went to young bars, told young jokes, and that disdain, which he had felt since he was at college and which had often impelled him to dress and act older than he was, now made it impossible for him to even contemplate the idea of going with Roberto now.

"So who is going to this party, tell me, who that I know?"

"No one, but they're really nice boys."

"Can't you see? That's the problem. They're nice *boys*."

"Well, I'm a *boy*, too," Roberto said, imitating the disdainful tone he had placed on the word.

"It's different with you."

"Oh, yeah? Why?"

He didn't want to be having that conversation and yet he knew that Roberto was taking him, maybe unintentionally, into the pit of his fear.

"It's different with you because you're older, really."

"I am no older or more mature than any of them, and they're my friends and I love them."

"I'm not telling you not to love them, or saying that they're not nice, I'm sure they are."

"But?"

"I don't know, Roberto."

"Look, all I know is that you've been acting strange ever since you got back from Barcelona. You have no idea what it took for me to get the night off and you don't seem to appreciate it at all, and I put flowers everywhere and you don't even notice."

There was a silence in which Roberto seemed to expect him to agree, and he didn't. Although he was right, he just looked at him without saying anything, praying silently that he would not go down that road.

"Plus, the tickets cost me eight thousand pesetas each," he concluded, almost whispering.

"If that's what you're worried about, you can take the money from my wallet."

"Don't be stupid."

Roberto started to get dressed, quickly, without looking at him.

"What are you doing?"

"I'm going."

"Well, then, don't come back. If you leave, don't bother coming back."

"You are a real asshole."

"Yes, I am."

Why was he doing that? Why was he sitting there, motionless, watching him get dressed, wearing that stupid, self-satisfied expression on his face, pretending he didn't care if Roberto left? What was he going to do now? Roberto put on his shoes and left the room. He heard him put on his coat by the door. He slammed the door when he left. He looked at the unmade bed, the glass Roberto had drunk out of, the ashtray full of butts, the flowers.

"Don't go," he said.

A second went by, and then another, and another, and with each passing second a void was accumulating, making a minute, then thirty, and then an hour when the sky turned a leaden gray, with no faces but with voices calling to each other on the street, laughing on their way to a party, maybe the one Roberto was going to. Twelve o'clock was just another minute, one when he heard the ruckus of a group of kids who had been taken by surprise under his window as the clock struck. Then the phone rang and he felt his blood run cold. He tripped over a piece of furniture as he ran to the living room to get it. It was Marta. Happy New Year, and did he want to come over, Ramón was there and the kids hadn't gone to bed yet. No, he didn't want to. He had a bad headache. Since he'd boarded the plane, ever since he'd boarded the plane his head had hurt terribly. He hung up. He thought about Roberto, but as if he'd never belonged to him, and he was afraid, again, to stop loving him, to stop being loved by him. He dressed quickly, without a clear idea of what he was going to do, and went out. He recalled that Roberto had once told him that he liked to go to the bars in Chueca so that's where he headed. It was too crowded and everyone was shouting. The annoying presence of happiness rejected him like a foreign body and he felt, suddenly, very old amongst all those drunk teenagers.

"Happy New Year!" a boy next to him cried, looking at him. "Cheer up, man, it's New Year's Eve!"

Roberto wasn't there. Or, rather, he was everywhere. A back, a similar coat, a voice. Every time he thought he saw him his heart would start to race. He'd tell him he was so sorry, that he had acted like an idiot, that he had been right, that he wasn't embarrassed of him, or of his friends, that it was just that he was scared. Could he understand that? Of course he could, he'd go to the damn party, they'd get drunk together, and then they'd go back home together. He wouldn't do it again, he swore he wouldn't do that again.

Roberto didn't appear. In his place, the night took on a cold, icy chill. The cars were all honking their horns in an infectious jubilation that seemed artificial. A boy vomited in the doorway of a bar. He went back home slowly, burdened by the unbearable weight of love.

He called him three times the next morning but got the answering machine each time. On his fourth attempt—it was almost two o'clock—Roberto's tired voice answered.

"Roberto . . ."

"Hello."

"Roberto, I'm so sorry, I acted like a complete idiot last night."

"Yeah."

His voice sounded tired, or disappointed, or sad.

"Do you want to come over? I bought champagne, and lamb. We can have lamb."

"I'm going home for dinner, with my sisters."

"You could come over afterwards."

"OK."

"Will you come?"

"Yes."

"What time?"

"I don't know, about eight."

"Eight? Can't you come any earlier?"

"No."

"OK, eight. Big kiss."

"Goodbye."

Roberto didn't come at eight. Or eight-thirty. Or nine. At nine fifteen he heard the elevator coming up, but there had already been so many false alarms that he didn't get excited until he heard it stop on his floor, and when it did, he didn't know what to do. He didn't know if he should run to the door or stay on the sofa, as he normally did. Roberto opened the door with his key and he got up. He walked over to him. Roberto's furrowed brow made him look strangely unattractive, like a child having a tantrum.

"I'm sorry," he said.

"You're an asshole."

"I know. Do you forgive me?"

"I guess."

They kissed. Within two hours Roberto's reservations seemed to have vanished completely and they were taking off their clothes in the bedroom. Roberto asked him what he'd done last night and he confessed that he'd gone out to look for him. This pleased Roberto and he wanted to hear every detail.

"You never would have found me in Chueca because I wasn't there, I was in Sol."

"Did you have fun?"

"No, everyone kept asking me what was wrong, why I wasn't dancing or anything."

"You didn't dance?"

"I didn't have anyone to dance with."

"I bet there were thousands of guys who were dying to dance with you."

"There were lots of guys, but I didn't want to dance with them."

Roberto was wearing lipstick, and his lips were so full and fleshy that they gave his whole face an almost fictional quality and he felt an almost religious devotion to him, as if he couldn't quite believe that this boy actually loved him.

He had that day off, and the next, and the following two as well. Since he'd worked an extra day in Barcelona, they were giving him a day in return. The joy of the night they made up turned out to be, in part, fictitious. It wasn't long before his fear, jealousy, anxiety returned. At times he even thought he would have been better off if he'd never met Roberto. He was tired of living in a constant state of agitation and some part of him missed the peace he'd felt in his years of resignation, when happiness was simple and had no consequence, when it was a tumbler of Napoleon cognac in his after-dinner daze, when it was expensive cigarettes, the odd dinner at an elegant restaurant.

Roberto's love moved him, and yet, ever since the night of the argument, it seemed as if something had broken; it wasn't the argument itself (which had been unimportant), but the consequences it had had. In the same way that sometimes a beautiful body stops being beautiful when put on display, Roberto's silence, like all things peaceful, could become intolerably boring. And yet beneath that "no" lay a passion for the "yes" that broke each time he observed Roberto's unwavering need to be a loving creature. Within his predictable form of loving—nothing could be as predictable as his kindness—youth at times conquered corporeality, the voluptuousness of a look, and that was when he became, once again, indecipherable.

One of those evenings, Roberto called one of his friends who worked at the Laundromat and they spoke for about fifteen minutes. Roberto had decided to make the call, in fact, because after sitting down next to him on the sofa, he didn't pay any attention. He was watching the news and, though it wasn't very interesting, Roberto's presence felt like an intrusion. Feeling rejected, Roberto had gone, without resentment, to make a phone call, and when he did, he couldn't stop looking at him. Roberto asked for Marcos and he thought he noted from the tone of the conversation that there was some degree of complicity between the two of them, jokes that he wouldn't understand and that, nevertheless, made Roberto laugh hysterically, carefree. The discomfort he felt watching Roberto laugh was too complex to be called simply "jealousy." That was the first time he became aware of the fact that there was a huge part of the twenty-one-year-old boy's life that he would never be a part of, and that he suddenly felt an urgent need to share. When had Roberto ever laughed that way with him? Why hadn't he? The boy who was on the phone (legs crossed, cigarette in the ashtray), was he Roberto or not? And if that was the real Roberto, then why did he have the impression that he didn't know him? Within a few seconds he became terrified by the idea that Roberto had tired of him. It all added up, it was a perfect syllogism: Roberto had never loved him, he had, at first, admired him, and later pitied him, so his love would only last as long as his admiration or his pity; he would never truly possess that boy who was laughing carefree, with bare feet and painted toenails, because he was not equal to him. What happened then was more than self-disdain, or the desire to be like someone else, to be someone else; what happened then is that he yearned to be the boy Roberto was talking to, to be twenty, to work at the Laundromat, to have to save up for a night at the theater, and for cigarettes, to make Roberto laugh like that.

"Who's that Marcos?"

"Oh, just a friend. We work together at the Laundromat. Why?"

"No reason."

He tried to feign indifference while still staring at the television but Roberto suddenly burst out laughing.

"Are you jealous of Marcos?"

"Me?"

"You're jealous of Marcos!" Roberto shouted, endlessly amused by the discovery, almost proud of having been able to incite jealousy. He felt stupid for having started the conversation and wanted to end it as quickly as possible, but he also wanted Roberto to squelch his fears, to tell him that Marcos was incredibly unattractive. And that feeling made him uncomfortable because he saw the childishness of his concern.

"You're jealous of Marcos!" Roberto repeated, standing in front of him so he could look into his eyes, still laughing.

"Stop it."

"You're jealous of Marcos!" Roberto repeated again, putting his hands on his legs so it was impossible not to look at him. He pushed Roberto off and jumped up suddenly.

"Well, so what? What if I am jealous, you damn fool."

Roberto stopped laughing immediately and opened his eyes wide. Roberto's enormous brown eyes, staring at him.

"Hey . . ." Roberto said.

"You don't understand anything," he said, storming off. But when he'd left the living room he didn't know what to do, so he headed for the bedroom.

"Hey . . ." Roberto said, walking in, with a tinge of sadness in his voice. He didn't turn around to look at him; that would have been too easy, too predictable.

"What."

He felt Roberto put his arms around him from behind.

"Marcos is just a guy I work with, I'm not interested in him at all, and he's had a girlfriend for the past three years. Don't get like this."

"Like what?"

"Please. Sometimes you're infuriating," Roberto said, removing his arms and going back to the living room. He heard him turn off the television and put on the Chopin record, which lasted only a few seconds because he took it off almost immediately and put on the modern music that he had once bought for him, and which, from the bedroom, he took to be the definitive sign of Roberto's no longer trying to please him. He was young, insultingly young, and always would be. That choice proved it. This was what he had feared ever since he'd started having this relationship with him; he had gotten tired of him, of putting up with him, he was suffocating, and so he was not surprised when Roberto came back into the bedroom and said he needed a break, just a few days, to think.

"Think about what?"

"About us, what do you think?" he said.

* * *

That night he hadn't cared about Roberto going home, but the following day he'd had to stop himself several times from dialing his number. Roberto had asked for four days, told him not to call, and though exhaustion had made him believe, at the time, that it wouldn't take much effort, in actuality not even one day had gone by and it was already torture.

The anxiety and nerves of the first day were followed by desperation on the second. He had gone to bed the night before repeating to himself, in an attempt to calm down, that Roberto was going to call him the next day and at five o'clock he was so nervous he hadn't been able to have lunch. He went down to walk the dog, who had become more unsociable than usual due to the lack of affection he'd received in the past couple of weeks. Roberto had said he wanted to think "about us." What a stupid expression. About us. It sounded like something out of a teenage miniseries. "To think about us," Roberto had said, as if he were on one of those stupid television series that he probably watched every day when he got home, like any other twenty-one-year-old boy. Roberto could be his son. That had occurred to him many times before, but at that moment the thought exceeded the limits of the grotesque. He could be Roberto's father. He didn't feel guilty then, he felt deceived; there had never, from the start, been any real reason for Roberto to complain about the way he'd behaved. He had always treated him to absolutely everything and never skimped on anything: the most expensive wine, the best meat, cigarettes. What did that boy have to complain about? About his not going to that party? Hadn't that been Roberto's own fault, really? He'd told him, right from the first, that he didn't want to go and, inverting roles, he didn't think he would ever have insisted on Roberto doing anything he had expressly and immediately said he really did not want to do. Really, he'd done it to test him.

But there was something in all of that that didn't add up. To believe that would have meant believing Roberto was shrewd, and wicked, which was something he also could not accept. He returned home at night, after the longest walk with the dog he could ever recall, starving. He fried up a couple of steaks and ate them almost violently, and then he went to bed. He couldn't sleep. He smoked three cigarettes in a row. He vomited.

The morning of the third day he felt exhausted, but also couldn't stand the idea of staying at home. Everything reminded him of Roberto. He called Marta and asked if he could come over for lunch.

"Of course . . . Are you okay?"

"Yes, I'm fine, I just feel like seeing you. Is that so strange?"

"No, of course not. Come, come on over, whenever you like."

In the time that passed while he was waiting for three o'clock to arrive, a strange destructive streak grew in him. He recalled years gone by with nostalgia, not because he

preferred solitude, nobody in their right mind preferred solitude, but because at least he knew where he stood with solitude. Reflecting on his condition filled him with a mixture
of displeasure and rage. And his picture of Roberto began
to take on an almost dangerous, threatening air. Now he
was afraid, not of Roberto falling out of love with him, but
of Roberto himself.

Marta was home alone. Ramón was working and the
kids wouldn't be home till six.

"Are you sure you're okay?"

"Why do you keep asking?" he replied, slightly irritated.

"Well, to be honest, because you never come over for
lunch on a weekday, just like that."

"Well I'm still on vacation, and since I couldn't see you
over New Year's . . ."

Marta, though she looked surprised throughout lunch
and kept asking about his health and his job in an attempt
to discover the real reason for the visit, finally gave in to the
idea that her brother had actually just come over because
he wanted to chat. Then when they were having coffee, she
suddenly smacked her forehead, as if she'd forgotten something unforgivable.

"You remember Uncle Juan?"

"Yes. Is he okay?"

"Is he okay? He's getting married!"

"How old is he now?"

"Sixty-three. But wait, that's not the best part. Get this:
the lucky bride-to-be is twenty-eight."

Marta interpreted his silence as a sign of the same incredulity that she must have felt on hearing the news, and this encouraged her.

"That's the same reaction I had. Dumbfounded."

"What does he say about it?"

"Who, Uncle Juan? Uncle Juan says they're in love, and really, maybe he is, but the girl? Personally, I think Uncle Juan is just rich and horny as hell, is all."

"Do you think it's impossible for two people with a big age difference to fall in love?"

Marta pursed her lips as a sign of physical displeasure, but since he didn't say anything she seemed to feel obliged to go into detail.

"Look, the way I see it, for an older person to fall in love with someone younger, that's not necessarily bad, because it happens all the time, let's not kid ourselves, it's normal, say, for a woman to fall in love with a younger guy, but she doesn't really fall in love with him, she just gets a crush, you know what I mean, but for a young girl to throw herself into the arms of an old man, that's just ugly, it's not natural, I don't know, just think about the girl in ten year's time, people will think it's his granddaughter taking him for a walk."

Lunch with Marta and especially the story about his uncle gave him a strange sense of peace that confirmed the impossibility of his relationship with Roberto, and then he felt overcome by a coldness that analyzed his relationship not as something disagreeable but something almost immoral, dirty, something he had fallen into as a result of having been lonely for so many years.

Roberto called the next day and he said that he was waiting for him, and to come over. When he saw him walk in, he observed the same signs of worry that he himself had: bags under the eyes, the tired-sounding voice, a contained sadness.

"Hello," Roberto said.

He had lost his charm; now Roberto was just a defeated boy he looked at, from the stature of his fifty-six years, almost condescendingly.

"Well. Did you think 'about us' or not?"

Roberto was so sad that he didn't even catch the irony in his words.

"Actually, I came for help, for you to tell me what I should do. I've been thinking about it so much, but . . ."

"You want to leave me, that's what you want to do, but you don't know how because you feel such pity for me. But you know what? I don't want anybody's pity, so you don't have to worry about it. I don't get you hot anymore, right? Isn't that how you say it nowadays? I don't get you hot. I used to get you hot, I don't know why, maybe it was morbid curiosity, but now you're bored, you won't admit it, of course, but I know. I'm not saying you don't feel anything at all for me, maybe a little affection, because you're either a very good liar or you feel something, but that's not enough for me, and if I say you don't understand me, it's because you don't understand me, how could you understand me, you'd have to have spent twenty years alone to understand me, alone, with nobody, for almost as many years as you've been alive, that's how long I've been alone. Have you ever thought about that? Tell me, have you ever thought about that?"

"Yes, of course I have," he said. "Why are you talking to me like that?"

"Well, if you've thought about that," he continued, trying not to lose his line of reasoning, "then you should have realized that you can't just turn up, the way you turned up, and ask me to become a twenty-one-year old, because that can't happen, Roberto, you can't ask me to go to some bar and get drunk as if I might want to do that because I don't. Before you came along I was used to my life, I had compensations, the little things that made me happy, and that was enough, and now it's going to take me five years to get over you. What about that? Did you ever think about that? You didn't, did you? And don't tell me you need another break and then come back a week later and tell me that you're leaving me. Just walk out the door and disappear if you want, but don't tell me you need another break. There. Now I've done all your work for you. What do you think?"

"I think you've said it all, it's all about you, and you didn't even really think about me," Roberto responded, his voice choked.

"Too much. I thought about you. Too much."

"It seems like you're asking me to leave you."

"I'm asking you to leave me because deep down that's what you really want to do, Roberto."

"You're asking me to leave you because I don't love you, but really, I'm going to leave you because I'm starting to realize that it's you who doesn't love me."

He didn't answer. Roberto's reply had struck him in the face, like a blow. The whole feeling of discursive, argumentative coherence that he thought he'd maintained throughout his speech was brought down by Roberto's few words. He took out his set of keys to the apartment and left them on the table by the front door. Then he put on his coat.

"I think you're a sad man," Roberto said as he turned around and closed the door slowly behind him, without the slam he'd been expecting.

The dog barked. He could hear the second hand of the living room clock tick as the elevator came to his floor, and the door opened, and Roberto got in. He stuck his head out the window and saw him walk out, stop, catch a bus. Outside, winter's chill cut to the bone.

DEBILITATION

SARA GOT OUT OF THE POOL the same way she always got out of the pool: attempting to quell the greasy feeling, the revulsion that her own wet body produced.

"You are something else. A body like that and you won't wear a bikini," said Teresa.

And Sara: "Whatever."

Luis hadn't stopped staring since the moment she took off her wrap and dove in, not stopping to rinse off first because she couldn't take the heat another minute. They hadn't exchanged a word since their kiss, a week before. It had all been so quick, so odd, that if she stopped to think about it now, it was disjointed in her memory: Luis's hands, his "I really like you," her glancing at her watch knowing they were going to be late to Teresa's birthday, and then the kiss; Luis's ridiculous, almost unpleasant tongue like a soggy worm wiggling against hers, her own excitement flaring up first like a burst of wonder and then of disgust when she felt him touch her chest. It wasn't that she didn't like Luis—she'd always liked Luis—it was the profound sense of repulsion she felt at the unexpected and unfamiliar reaction of her own body, which was a sort of tension and swelling, a sort of pleasure, but unarticulated pleasure, which she felt again now as she got out of the pool that she and Teresa had been invited to, and it almost made her wish she hadn't dived in to begin with so that she wouldn't now have to go running—acting like nothing was the matter—back to her towel to shield herself from Luis's gaze, Luis's friend's gaze, even Teresa's gaze as her friend repeated that if she had Sara's body she'd wear not one bikini but a thousand, and Luis nodded vigorously while at the same time seeming, perhaps, to reproach her for the fact that they still hadn't spoken about what happened a week earlier.

She felt the towel around her waist like a welcome reprieve, and didn't take it off for the rest of the afternoon. Classes were starting in a week and the end of that summer was tinged with a tired pink indolence. She'd spent one month at the beach with her father, and the month of August in Madrid with her mother. Although it had been three years since their divorce, her mother was still inhabiting an emotionally precarious state that, from the start, had led Sara to side with her and against her father, who for over a year she continued to see as a hostile enemy. It was different now. She was sixteen and had been held back a year but it didn't really matter. Throughout her childhood Sara had been a big girl, which is why—though she had never been overly talkative and her silence, most of the time, concealed plain and simple shame—during that time she took great satisfaction in her own physical strength. But adolescence changed things. Not only did she stop growing, but in a little under a year and a half she also turned into a first-class beauty. She could tell more by others' reactions to her than by her own. Sara herself felt that by losing stature, or rather by the other girls at school becoming the same height, she was also losing her confidence, her respectability. What for others was a perfect smoothing out of edges that seemed were never going to lose their clumsy shape, she experienced as a sort of debilitation. The emergence of her breasts, the accentuation of her waist, was all a sort of sliminess, a liquefaction, and which is why her pleasure at feeling strong was substituted by the pleasure she took in being rude, in silence.

She took it almost as praise when her mother said that she was unfeminine, and though well-groomed, she never worried about how she dressed, and cut her hair like a boy's so as not to waste time styling it.

That worked for three years. Until Luis. It had all worked perfectly until Luis, and it's not that she hadn't liked kissing Luis, it wasn't a matter of liking it or not liking it, but of the feeling—almost identical—that she'd experienced again when getting out of the pool, a feeling that wasn't shame or weakness or disgust, though it contained an element of all three. They'd been talking about what they wanted to study at university, after finishing high school that year.

"What about you, Sara? What do you want to do?"

"I don't know. I haven't thought about it."

"But isn't there anything you at least like?"

"I like to draw."

"Draw," Luis's friend said, with a slightly sardonic tone, and she shot daggers at him.

"Yes, draw. I like to draw," she replied, and the kid didn't open his mouth again.

Teresa asked her later, as they were getting dressed in the changing room, why she'd been so rude to the guy, and she didn't know what to say. She was amazed at the ease, almost complacency, with which Teresa, whose body was more developed than her own, undressed.

"The thing is," she said, "I really like this guy, and if you keep acting like that you're going to scare him off. He doesn't seem like it, but he's shy—what? Are you into me, or what?"

"What do you mean?"

"You were staring."

"No," Sara replied almost blushing, because it was true: the white skin under Teresa's bikini, against her deep summer tan, lent a strange luminescence to her breasts and crotch, and combined with the nonchalant way she'd taken off her bathing suit, it took on a kind of power, a resolve that hypnotized Sara. Teresa wasn't pretty, but her body, unlike Sara's, seemed complete; even the curves of her hips and breasts had an architectonic grace that made her attractive.

Luis waited for Sara, hoping to ride the bus home with her, but she asked him to leave, so she could think about things. *Think about things* was the expression Sara used when, rather than actually think about something, she wanted to sink into a state of semi-conscious vacuousness in which images, words, and plans flew by one after another with no logic, like objects seen from the window of a train.

"So it didn't mean anything to you," Luis concluded.

"What?"

"Last week."

"No," Sara replied.

"Got it," Luis said, walking off.

Sara took the bus back and got off two stops early in order to walk through the park. One word was pounding in her temples. It was a simple word, perfect and white. It was in the trees, in the joggers' breath, in the sudden warm dark of that September night. Several times she almost said it out loud. Her mother wasn't home when she got in. From beneath their apartment came the sounds of the outdoor café near the door to their building. She went into the bathroom and took off all her clothes in front of the mirror. Before her there appeared a reflection, the figure of a girl who, in the shadow of the bathtub, resembled a white breastplate, an Amazon prepared for battle. The word she'd been dreaming of all afternoon bubbled up, effervescent, from some hidden place, deep down, and Sara smiled at her naked reflection.

"Control," she whispered.

The world froze stock-still for a few seconds, like a virgin ashamed of a dream. It was September 2.

The line separating the Sara that was from the one she would become from that moment on couldn't have been finer. It seemed there had in fact been no change, that everything had stopped for an instant only to carry on from another point, Sara still being Sara, like the unthinkable reaction of an acquaintance which, upon reflection, not only stops being unthinkable but actually seems logical, coherent. Control was change, change was control, and both were a void filled with images that led nowhere. And nothingness was desirable. And in nothingness, everything could simply be discovered. And Sara saw that it was good.

She bumped into Luis close to home a week after classes started. He was uneasy, and his uneasiness ended up rubbing off on her.

"Listen, Sara," he said, fidgeting with his hands, "I've been thinking . . . I don't know, I mean, to me, what happened that day meant something . . . I just wanted you to know."

"Okay."

"Well?"

"Well what?"

"Fine," Luis concluded hastily. "I guess that's life, right?"

"Whose life?" she asked, and it was Luis, then, who turned strangely solemn.

"Goodbye, Sara."

It was late and she went up to the apartment to make dinner. She wasn't thinking about Luis when she opened the door, or when she dropped her books in her room, or when she began peeling potatoes in the kitchen to make a meat stew. Her mother wasn't home yet. She worked at a newspaper and sometimes got home late. Sara loved her the way one loves a deaf dog, or a bored child gazing out the window at a park.

Suddenly it occurred to her. She recalled a few conversations about it with Teresa's friends, even Teresa herself. She recalled, also, that she'd felt a kind of repugnance, not for them but for their smugness. She went to the bathroom and undressed from the waist down. Sitting on the bidet, she began to touch herself. The displeasure she at first felt was overcome the moment she realized that it was the same sense of repulsion she'd felt while kissing Luis but now different, because something about it seemed pleasurable. Sara felt a body inside her own body come into being, a body that understood Luis, and her mother, and Teresa—a body she didn't like. Her pleasure was sharp and sustained for a few seconds and then gradually subsided. She washed her hands and put her clothes back on. She'd left the kitchen door open and the whole apartment was filled with the smell of stew. It was late, and she put on her pajamas after dinner. In her diary she wrote: *dear diary, today I masturbated.* Mamá still wasn't home. She was sad. And didn't know why.

October crept in the way October always creeps in. Having been held back a grade, Sara didn't know her new classmates very well, and having made zero effort to get close to them the first month of school, she'd ended up in the back row, playing the voluntary outcast, albeit with a little respectability due to her age. She saw Teresa between classes and at lunchtime, when they rode the bus home together. That day they did so in silence. Teresa had started going out with Luis's friend a few weeks earlier, which translated into them speaking less.

"Um, Sara," Teresa said with the deliberation of a long-avoided pronouncement. "You're acting weird."

She didn't reply.

"You're acting like you don't care about anything. I mean, you've always been kind of quiet, but now it's like you hardly even talk. Maybe . . . I don't know, maybe you think we're all boring, or maybe none of the other girls are smart enough for you." Sara's silence made Teresa change her tone, which became increasingly reproachful. "Or maybe you're just jealous of me because I have a boyfriend."

Teresa stopped to gauge her reaction, and Sara forced herself not to smile.

"No," she said, "that's not it."

"Then what is it? Luis?"

She was surprised Teresa even knew about that, but said nothing.

"Plus it's pretty messed up that I had to find out about it from him and not you. I mean—what? You don't trust me, or what? I mean, that's what friends are for, you know? 'The other day I got together with Sara,' he says yesterday, and I'm sitting there like an idiot pretending I've known all along, obviously, defending you, though I don't know why if you don't even tell me anything."

"You don't have to defend me, Tere," she said to shut her up.

"Fine. Do what you like," she responded, offended.

"Don't get mad."

"I'm not getting mad."

They sank back into silence. Teresa stood when they got to her stop.

"And as for Luis," she said, getting off the bus, "you should at least call him, or write to him. You can't just up and leave people like that, all cold-hearted."

"Okay," she replied.

Sara didn't write Luis nor did she call him, but the fact that she didn't write him or call him didn't mean she didn't think it was the right thing to do, it simply meant she wouldn't have known what to tell him, aside from the truth: that she didn't care about him. As the weeks went by it all built up inside her like some ball of dissatisfaction that, lacking an object on which to project itself, turned against her. First she felt despicable for not caring about him, but that only lasted a few days. Then she thought that sooner or later some other boy she actually did like would appear, but that, too, struck her as unlikely. Finally what materialized intact, redoubled, was that feeling of repulsion for her own body. "It's my period," she thought, but it continued in the weeks that followed. Sara disliked her period the way she disliked any other form of excretion, including her own sweat. She sprayed on cheap cologne twice a day for fear of smelling bad, but she couldn't stand perfume, either. It would have been ideal to have no smell.

Sometimes Sara dreamed she was invisible, that she got out of bed and wandered around the park without anyone perceiving her presence. When she woke up, the memory of that weightlessness would make her smile and she'd close her eyes to hold onto it for a few more seconds, but instead the awareness of her body made her bitter, and she'd usually give up in annoyance.

It was October twenty-eighth and windy the first time Sara used her mother's letter-opener (so pretty—gold, embossed with three bronze turtles) to make cuts on her legs. She was home alone and her mother wouldn't be back until late. She could hear the murmur of the television in the living room, distant. She tried to recall what she'd gone in there for when she saw it on the desk, next to some mail from the bank. That wasn't where it belonged. She stroked the tip carefully, almost sorrowfully. It was Tuesday and yet seemed more like it should have been a Thursday, or a Saturday, the night so bright with lights. She slid it down softly until the tip was against her thigh, then pressed the handle harder and harder. Sara watched it pierce the thin material of her pajamas, sink slightly into her skin. The pain was sharp, concentrated, simple. She realized her heart was racing as a spot of blood encircled the tip of the letter-opener, which was still stabbing into her leg. She didn't enjoy the pain but she could take it. She got the impression, at that moment, that the leg bleeding there was not her own but that of some weak and distant enemy for whom she must show no mercy. Without her pressing the tip any further in, the bloodstain spread into a perfect circle, a sun of blood. When Sara stopped pressing down and placed the letter-opener back on the desk she felt woozy. And then smiled. She'd won; she didn't know against what or whom.

Wednesday came, and Thursday and Friday, and on each of them the ceremony of the letter-opener was repeated like a simple, age-old ritual that had to be performed with absolute accuracy. Sara accepted it the way one accepts an ancient religion. If she knew her mother wasn't going to come home she did it right there, beside the desk, but if she was home, Sara would take the letter-opener, go to her room, close the door and turn the music up loud so that her mother wouldn't call her. Beside the wound from the first day—a dark spot, purplish around the edge—came others, some of them more superficial, most of them much like the first. Because she didn't know how long she'd spent pressing the tip into her flesh the first time, she decided she would do it for ten minutes. Sometimes, if she did it on her bare leg, she balked, because that made her more conscious of what she was doing. And yet once the first five minutes had gone by, she lost all awareness and it felt like plunging the letter-opener into a hunk of inanimate white flesh, into a ball of wax.

Just as most of life's events are of no significance, Sara didn't expect this one to be much different. The fact that she did it didn't mean she liked the pain. A pain produced voluntarily and which led to a feeling of pointlessness, of absurdity; but if she kept at it a little, waited for sensation to eclipse the threshold of reason, then came a pleasant state of self-possession, of control.

This feeling of self-possession, of hardening, put her in a good mood during those weeks, and yet her happiness, like all happiness, could not be shared. Who would understand? Her mother? Her father? Luis? One afternoon, on the way home from school, she was on the verge of telling Teresa, but right before doing so recalled the day they'd undressed together in the changing room at the pool and stopped immediately. No, Teresa wouldn't understand either, Teresa would get scared, think she was crazy, maybe even call her mother and tell her. Sara was afraid her happiness would be stolen from her, would be misinterpreted, and her fear grew deeper, and denser. The decision not to say anything to Teresa led to the decision not to tell anyone, ever, and the realization that it was a secret made Sara fear someone would find out. She began to hide and to embrace her happiness with a sort of angst that inevitably made her feel guilty. But guilty about what, before whom, she wondered.

Her father had been overly affable all weekend long. He'd asked too many questions about her classes and her girlfriends, kissed her too many times. Then he'd told her that

he'd met a woman, Sandra was her name, and that sometimes in life you had to take stock of things and try to start
fresh. They were at her grandparents' house in a small town,
just the two of them, and Sara had spent the morning on a
long walk. Wandering into town, which was no more than
two kilometers away, she'd witnessed a bizarre scene: a feral
dog had gotten onto someone's property and was mounting
a female dog chained to a doghouse. The bitch was trying
to escape but the male held her in place, trapped beneath
his paws. There were times in a man's life, her father said,
when it wasn't easy to be alone, and then when you least
expected it, someone just came along, someone who made
everything seem worthwhile again. The dog's claws were
black and curved, as was its insistence on penetrating her.
The bitch's eyes were watering. He was talking about tenderness, *ten-der-ness,* he said, drawing out each syllable as if
to give the word a deeper warmth. She threw a rock at the
male. A heavy black rock that filled the palm of her hand.
It struck the dog's rump softly and he let out a quiet whimper, followed by a guttural, slobbery growl, but didn't stop
mounting the bitch. She'd understand one day, too, maybe
not now, maybe not right this instant, but she'd see, the
years would go by and one day she'd recall that afternoon
and think: now I understand what my father meant. So she
grabbed another rock, a bigger one, and with all the force
she could muster hurled it over the fence. She missed. She
was more mature than other girls her age, so she shouldn't
be embarrassed about it or let anyone make fun of her. He'd

been lucky enough to learn what life was all about before it was over, yes, that's what he'd been—lucky. She tried with a long stick she found on the ground by her feet; shoving it through the fence, she began striking him on the muzzle. The male stopped mounting the female at that point and lunged for the fence like a fury. Sara jumped back, terrified, but when she realized the dog couldn't do anything she approached again and kicked the fence. Her heart was pounding. Your heart always pounds when you know you've found the person you've been looking for, but you had to be careful, it wasn't just a question of feelings, you had to be compatible too, because with her mother, it didn't matter how much they'd loved each other—and they'd loved each other so much—in the end there'd been nothing they could do except admit they couldn't live together, and that wasn't sad, it was just life. The barking made the owner come out of his house and scare off the dog who, before taking flight, turned to her to growl one last time.

"I'm going to the kitchen for more coffee. You want anything?"

"No."

"Good girl," said her father, and smiled wide, showing all his teeth.

That afternoon Sara waited on the balcony overlooking the park for the sky to take on the appearance of what it is: an enormous, empty blue backdrop. She loved that, especially as November approached. Autumn spread over the park like a beautiful disrobing. She hadn't seen or spoken to Teresa in two weeks, and the space her friend had occupied, which for the first few days had seemed so makeshift, so replaceable, ended up taking on a leaden consistency. She missed her. She phoned three times that afternoon without catching her at home and then, ten minutes after her third try, Teresa called back. She let her down. Sara had thought Teresa was her friend, and Teresa let her down.

"I can't go out with you later because I'm meeting Javier," she said. "Well, now that I think about it, there's going to be other people there too; Luis is coming . . . It's probably better if we go out another time."

"Fine." Sara's voice came out cold, unmodulated, as though irked that the conversation had lasted even that long.

"Aren't you going out with Teresa?" her mother asked after she hung up.

"No."

She thought she was going to cry, so she walked out of the room, put on her coat, and went down to the park. Sara always went down to the park when she didn't know what to do. It wasn't just that she liked going for walks but also the tingling sense of danger that rose in her throat when she went there late. A lot of things happened there at night.

"Drug addicts," her mother said, "bad people. They leave the gates open and people just go in and kill each other like animals."

It was like straddling two worlds: the daytime one, with couples and lovers and children, and this other one, the nighttime one, which sometimes appeared on the news because of rapes and overdoses, or in the doorwoman's frightened eyes as she recounted—crossing herself—what went on there.

Sara recalled one time she'd seen them pull a dead body from the lake. That was two years ago, one August morning, very early, when she'd gone for a walk. There was no one out and it was hot. She approached, drawn by the police car's lights. It was only a second, but she remembers perfectly his purple face, a T-shirt that said USA. She remembers that he had a bare foot—just one—and that that seemed somehow violent, and grotesque, and almost impossible. She remembers dreaming about the man many times, about the strange beauty of that man hoisted out with ropes which pulled him to the railing that bordered the walking path, the man whose body, as it was lowered over the rim, inexplicably flopped its head toward her in what had seemed like a voluntary movement, beautiful and hideous at the same time, calling to her.

That afternoon, everything was painful—the air, the dogs, the lovers—as though swept in from that August of the drowned man. She walked slowly toward the lake. It was Sunday, so the paths were crowded with clowns, guitarists, puppeteers.

"Where could that witch be?" asked a puppet.

"Over there!" a chorus of children shrieked, pointing.

"Where?"

"There!"

There was a dark heavy quality to the lake and, though

it was cold out, couples were still renting rowboats. Four, five couples, all of their faces tinged with a sort of grayish weariness, an age-old tedium. Sara sat down to watch them. She wanted to cry but contained herself. The discovery of her own fragility, her need for Teresa, had once more left her confronting a person who resembled her without being her, a person she once more reviled. She got cold but did not button up her coat. Icy air blew in through the cuffs of her jacket and pierced her sweater and shirt, hardening her. She was made of stone now. Hard as stone, she thought.

She stopped using the letter-opener to puncture her leg because it no longer took any effort, and because, since her conversation with Teresa, even that didn't make her feel better. She still went school in the mornings and came home alone at lunchtime. Her hardness, the feeling of being almost impervious to the things going on around her, was replaced by a sort of falling apart when she got home, went into her bedroom, and found herself alone. Sara felt so fragile she thought that anyone could have shattered her with nothing but the sound of their voice. Those feelings, though intense, were not prolonged, and after they subsided Sara felt an immeasurable desire to hurt herself, to test the limits of her endurance. Her body appeared before her then as total potential for change, an enormous project or an immense block of marble within which lay a precious sculpture.

She stopped eating one Wednesday that seemed it had

arrived from long ago, from childhood perhaps, because—just like in childhood—there was a surreal, fictitious happiness to it. She was alone in the kitchen and had heated up some leftover chicken thighs from the previous night's dinner, but when she opened the microwave and saw them steaming in shiny mucous Sara was overcome by a sudden, involuntary wave of nausea. She tossed the chicken in the trash and, though she was hungry, ate nothing. Her stomach rumbled for half an hour, at the end of which, after a few minutes of mild irritation, she no longer felt hungry.

That night her mother got home earlier than normal and announced that they were going out to dinner with Aunt Eli. Aunt Eli was her mother's sister and they'd always gotten along exceedingly well. Sara admired her Aunt Eli because she'd never married, because she lived in Barcelona, which was so cosmopolitan, so clean and civilized, with all those Gaudis everywhere. Aunt Eli was a civil engineer and always smelled like a brand of lotion you couldn't buy in Spain. Aunt Eli was happy.

Her mother tried to persuade Aunt Eli to go a restaurant close to home but she flatly refused and said that, if she was the one treating, she got to pick. They took a taxi to an elegant restaurant, one of those kinds of places she probably went to all the time.

"This is so expensive," her mother said, but no more had she finished her sentence than Eli, with a single sweep of first her hand and then her whole arm, had hushed her, signaled the waiter, and headed—as though floating through all the people—to a table in one corner that bore a handwritten *Reserved*.

"You're still wearing the sun charm I gave you," she said.

"I am," Sara replied happily, and they smiled at one another, each imagining that their smiles communicated many things that most people would have tried to explain but that they, wisely, preferred leave unspoken.

Work was the excuse Aunt Eli had used, but none of them was fooled as to why she'd made the trip. Ever since Sara's mother had discovered that her ex had a new girl-friend, she'd been oscillating between the languid, lazy *tristesse* she'd sunken into and occasional tears and nervous breakdowns which generally manifested in cleaning out the most unimaginable closets and storage spaces. Aunt Eli had come to save her mother, Sara thought.

Through most of dinner the only sound was that of Aunt Eli's voice as she recounted a trip to London, how marvel-ous London was and how terribly behind the times we in Spain were; how elegant British English was compared to the English they spoke in the US, or at least in New York (which she said in English, just like that, *New York*, like it was no big deal); and especially how astonishingly well she'd been treated everywhere she went. She accompanied each anecdote with a gesture that was simultaneously simple, practiced, elegant, and inimitable, and it struck Sara that if Aunt Eli were stripped naked and placed upon a table, the whole of her would gleam like a Lladró figurine.

Sara went to the bathroom and, on her return, found

them talking about her father. Her mother, recounting how she found out, and how she felt, wore a pathetic stifled expression that barely concealed her obvious urge to cry. Aunt Eli listened in silence, fingers interlaced beneath her chin, their bones illuminated in the faint light. As soon as her mother, whom Sara was starting to feel almost embarrassed for, finished talking, Aunt Eli would set things straight, tell her mother to stop being weak, teach her how to get over it.

But Aunt Eli, inexplicably, said nothing. Her mother, who also seemed surprised by this, kept talking.

"You should get out more, try to cheer up," Aunt Eli said finally, almost timidly.

"I've tried," her mother said, "believe me, I've tried. I thought I was doing better compared to a year ago, but now there's no place I can go without thinking: I'm going to bump into them, now I'm going to bump into them and then what do I do? Sara can tell you. Before, when he came to pick her up, he used to come upstairs, we'd chat; now he just buzzes from downstairs. 'Come on up,' I say, and he'll say, 'No, I can't, I'm in a hurry,' or whatever."

"I'd like to be able to say something that would cheer you up, and a month ago I think I would have, but I'm in more or less the same position."

"Wait. You?" her mother asked, surprised, voicing Sara's surprise as well.

"Remember how a year ago," she elaborated, "I used to go down to Málaga all the time, I said we had a bridge project going there? Well, it wasn't a bridge, it was a man named Ramón. He was separated then, had three daughters—he's a dentist. We went out all year. He asked me to marry him. I said no."

There came a long silence during which Sara wished she weren't there, wished she hadn't heard what she'd heard. Her incredulity vanished when she discovered that Aunt Eli, too, wore that same expression of helplessness, of weakness.

"Do you regret it?" her mother asked, and she felt blood rushing to her temples; no, she didn't regret it, she didn't.

"I went to Málaga to see him a couple of weeks ago. He was unhappy, you could tell. He told me he'd gotten back together with his wife. Do I regret not having married him? Yes, actually I do," said Aunt Eli as though talking to herself. "Maybe ten years ago I wouldn't have regretted it, but now? I do."

Her mother stroked her sister's back slowly, comfortingly.

"Quite the night for secrets, isn't it?" she concluded, attempting to smile, and then they both turned to her as though suddenly shy, as though ashamed of having laid themselves bare.

Aunt Eli died in Sara's imagination like an orchid whose cerulean beauty has weathered twenty long days and then, suddenly, shriveled in a single night, reduced to a horrible, wilted excrescence. That was exactly the way Aunt Eli had died no pride, no class. If Sara behaved strangely the rest of the night, it was only because she felt deceived. How could she have admired that woman so much? A woman who suddenly admitted her ridiculous weakness, pressed her hands to her stomach, wore an expression of sharp pain, took an antacid.

She went to bed that night with an oddly empty feeling, recalling Aunt Eli's words over and over. She was alone now, definitively, there was no turning back. It was like having witnessed the death of a god, of God.

First it was just dinner. A week later, breakfast too. Two weeks after that almost all food. In the space of that first month she lost twelve pounds. Her mother said repeatedly that she looked thin, she had to eat more. Sara would agree immediately, and this response—so immediate, so compliant—would of course crush the conversation. Her father, too, reproached her from time to time, though the only consequence was being subjected to constant surveillance during the occasional meal.

Sara, in turn, discovered an unknown world within the one she thought she knew. The physical discomfort of hunger (which was, incidentally, so easy to outwit) seemed a risible price to pay for the pleasure obtained from fasting. She woke up tired and was exhausted by the slightest physical effort, but in exchange the world became bearable, weightless, almost dignified. Sara floated from her bed to the bus, from the bus to class, to the whispering in class, and then again, on her way home, walked through the park, the December cold in her face, and she felt restored. It was as if everything came alive beneath her skin.

But it wasn't just the weightlessness. Her fight to overcome that most basic of needs, for the first time in a very long time, made her feel superior. It was a competition against herself and everyone else—holding out until hunger, after a secretion of juices, became a concentrated pain in an identifiable place in her stomach. She'd prepare miniscule packets of food—cherry tomatoes, half a pear, half of a sandwich with the crusts cut off—and wrap them carefully in foil as if they were the last remaining provisions of a survivor. She ate them only when sensing that she was about to faint from weakness, and on doing so felt not a sense of relief but of it being a necessary evil, the vexatious obligation to subsist.

On the electronic scale in her mother's bathroom, she admired the results of her battle each day: 118.6 became 115.5; 115.5 became 110.1. Then the process went slower, got harder, but a nine turning to an eight meant going to bed with the joy of one who has finally rid themselves of something troublesome; liberation and control was nine becoming eight, and was also the hope that eight would turn to seven, six, nothing, air, as though she were voyaging to a land yet to be invented and each step were smaller and harder to take.

That hardness also had eyes and hands, and color, and feelings upon which to rest, but they were nothing like those she'd felt before. What she encountered now, each time she went out, was a world that was clear and systematizable, even if it appeared chaotic, a world in which not only did her loneliness matter less but her loneliness was in fact that which allowed her to better see the world, and judge it. Sometimes she got the feeling, as she walked out of the park and onto the wide avenue leading to her street, that she was actually the one directing that absurd concert of horns, voices, and buses. She'd stand still and stare fixedly at a person or thing and silently command its next move, and the people complied without even realizing it, without knowing they were in fact obeying her orders. When that happened, she got the sense that something simple and empty inside her fit perfectly—like the wooden blocks at nursery schools whose geometric shapes fit into holes—and the rising tide of sensations became even more powerful. Also: there were no words there. Control was as silent as a Monday night, more so, more silent even than that, as silent as eyes gliding slowly over the words in a book.

Unstitching her trouser seams to resew them so you couldn't tell was one strategy she used to disguise her weight loss those first months. It worked until Christmas dinner. Aunt Eli and her grandmother had come, like always, and—not having seen her in months—both erupted in exclamations from the start. Sara detested them the moment they started in.

"Trying to look like one of those models on TV doesn't make you more attractive, you know," said Aunt Eli.

And her grandmother:

"Good God, child, have you seen yourself in the mirror? You look like you could be swept off by the wind."

They were having lamb for dinner. She realized that in the past three weeks, she hadn't eaten a single bite of meat. It wasn't that she didn't like lamb, she'd always liked lamb, but as soon as dinner preparations had begun, as soon as her mother put the lamb in the oven and the kitchen filled with the aroma of roasting meat, she knew she wasn't going to be able to eat it. When they sat down at the table and her mother asked for her plate to serve her, Sara wavered for a second, then turned her eyes to the platter where the carved rack lay steaming, felt nauseous and said: "I can't."

"Can't what?" her mother asked.

"I can't eat meat; I'm a vegetarian."

"Since when, may I ask?"

"A month ago."

"That's not healthy, it can't be healthy," her grandmother said.

"So why haven't you said anything all month?"

"I don't know."

"Margarita, Carmen's friend, she was a vegetarian, you could hardly stand to look at her," her grandmother continued.

"No. *I don't know* is not an answer."

"She was always fainting, white as a sheet of paper."

"I didn't tell you because I wasn't sure myself until now, that's why."

"You see?" her mother said to Aunt Eli. "See how she doesn't tell me anything?"

"That doctor on TV, the one who comes on after lunch,

he always says how important it is to eat meat," said her grandmother.

"Sara," said Aunt Eli, "it's not that being a vegetarian is bad; I myself was a vegetarian for a few years, but . . ."

"And I could hardly stand to look at you, all the weight you lost. And you got those dizzy spells, don't forget," her grandmother carried on.

"But what matters is that you talk about things."

"And eat meat."

"Mamá, be quiet a minute, you're putting my nerves on edge," her mother said.

"Tell me to be quiet, fine, you and your sister both want me to die."

"Nobody wants you to die," said Aunt Eli.

"Then why are you always telling me to be quiet?"

"Sara, you have to eat," her mother said.

"We were talking about Sara," Aunt Eli replied.

"So was I, you'd know that if you listened to me."

"Being a vegetarian is fine, if that's what you want, but you have to make sure to get plenty of iron: lentils, garbanzos . . ."

"Protein, meat."

"Mamá, please!" her mother shouted.

"Don't you raise your voice at me!" her grandmother shouted back.

"Be quiet!" Sara yelled. "All of you, just be quiet! You drive me crazy!"

She got up and ran to her room, slammed the door, and

locked it. Lying on her bed she pressed her hands to her ears, hard, wanting to disappear, to be miniscule, small as an insect that could scurry under doors, small as a speck of dust.

She didn't answer when her mother knocked on the door, or when she asked her to please come back to the table, or when she returned ten minutes later begging, saying that it was Christmas dinner, or when she said she was leaving some salad and fruit by the door and that she didn't have to come out if she didn't want to but, please, just eat something. Sara remained motionless, hands clamped tightly to her ears, first consciously, then as if her arms no longer belonged to her, hearing the sound of her heartbeat, her breathing, in her palms. It was an uncomfortable position but she didn't move. She needed to stay that way: still. Opening her eyes, she saw the mattress and the poster of Renoir's ballerina, white and weightless, as though made of perfume. She could sleep that way, too, eyes open, on tiptoe.

On the refrigerator was a vegetarian meal plan, dreamed up by her mother and Aunt Eli. Beside each food, in a different color, its protein content. Monday to Sunday, not a single dish repeated: lentils were followed by asparagus, eggs, garbanzos, all in perfect order, an order that by mere virtue of its existence, could not be accepted.

Sometimes Sara skipped class. She knew full well which

subjects her absences would likely go unnoticed in and took advantage of this in order to go to the park, a place she'd begun to find strangely fascinating. She'd always liked the park and as a girl had spent long afternoons there, but now it felt different, like a gloomy extension of herself. Crossing the whole of it on a regular weekday—without any of the Sunday and holiday commotion—was like traversing a vast, unreal space, a space that was at once desert-like and yet intimate and recognizable, it was like thinking about a song that made you sad. Sara was the air and trash, the grass and the empty puppet stand, and most of all—the lake. If she didn't at first realize, it was only because ending up there always seemed like a coincidence, because when she suddenly caught sight of it—placid and simple as a ring of water—she got the feeling she hadn't consciously headed there and had simply bumped into the lake along her way.

She immersed her awareness into it, sitting on the grass, always at the same spot. Contemplating its round heavy density, from her own place of lightness, was pleasing and yet at the same time devoid of significance. Standing up, gazing at it for the last time, trudging slowly back home was a form of surrender to another fear. Ever since Christmas vacation ended and she'd had to go back to school, Sara had felt like everyone was staring at her in the same sort of shock, which could be interpreted as anything from commiseration to pure and simple disgust. In class, where her presence had always gone undetected, kids started playing jokes on her. One day when she sat down, she discovered that someone had drawn a skeleton on her desk, and the girls who sat beside her sometimes angled their chairs away slightly so as not to have to see her.

Sara would have been distraught if any of that had seemed real, if the people who said things seemed real, but for weeks all that was real was the lake, her bedroom ceiling. Even her mother seemed unreal. If Sara was in the living room and heard her mother come in from work, she got the feeling that it was all absurd, that something incomprehensible and utterly absurd was happening.

"What are you doing here?" she'd ask.

"What do you mean what am I doing here? I just got in from work. What's the matter with you?"

"Nothing. I was just thinking."

Her mother, for her part, had fallen into a whiny sort of apathy the first week after vacation, and all of her time at home seemed to revolve around getting Sara to eat. Often, especially while in the kitchen getting dinner ready—something Sara had stopped doing ages ago—her mother talked to herself, cursing the fact that she always put others first, lamenting having no one to take care of her. Her complaints—at first mumbled under her breath, later mindlessly repeated like the words of someone unable to remember why they're doing whatever they're doing—formed part of what was now a nightly monologue. That particular night, though, was different.

"I saw them," her mother said.

"Who?"

"Who do you think? Your father and that Sandra woman . . ."

"So what?" Sara asked indifferently.

"So *what*? They were having dinner at the very restaurant where we used to celebrate our anniversary."

In silence, Sara despised the weakness of this woman who was her mother, this woman who didn't stop blathering until she'd described every detail of the encounter. She despised her choked tone, her pallor, the purplish bags under her eyes, her shoes. She despised everything around her—the comfort of the sofa they were sitting on, the indoor plants, the Discobolus her father had brought back from Greece that now had magazines piled behind it, the photo of her grandfather, the expensive painting hanging over the TV.

"So, what do you think?"

"I think you're weak," Sara replied slowly, "and you're not actually suffering that much."

"You're not serious."

Sara was about to reply that she was.

"No," she said.

Although it lasted only a second, they would both remember that silence. It was as though in that moment they'd finally come to know each other, as though they'd never truly seen each other before.

"I'm going to bed," Sara said, "I'm tired."

"It's only eight-thirty," her mother replied.

She didn't turn to look at her. She walked out of the

living room the way you walk out of a stranger's house, an uncomfortable house, and closed her bedroom door. So many pointless things there, too: so stupid, the look on her dolls' faces; so facile and pathetic, the pink curtain, her bedspread, the picture of her and Teresa at camp. She grabbed a plastic bag and began to stuff all the things she didn't need into it. Books were too heavy, so she piled those by the door. When she was finished, satisfied, she looked around at the bare walls. She hadn't eaten a bite all day and the physical effort had made her lightheaded. She heard her mother whimpering into the phone, saying she didn't know what to do with her anymore. Then she came to Sara's door and stood outside it without knocking. Sara could hear her there breathing, like an enemy attempting to rob her of the whiteness, the lovely new simplicity in her object-less room.

"Sweetheart," she said. "Sara . . ."

Sara didn't answer. Answering would have been a predictable capitulation.

"Sweetheart. I know you're going through a tough time right now. Let me help you."

Her last sentence had been spoken with the uncertainty of someone reciting a line they'd been fed. Those words weren't hers. Of course they weren't hers.

"I'm going through a tough time, too; we can help each other."

Sara gazed at her open hands, holding them out before her, and was aghast at how ugly they were. A blue vein, which crisscrossed near her fingers, ran up the back of her hand to her wrist and then disappeared, as though entering a tiny blue cave on her forearm.

"Let's both put in a little effort, Sara."

Her elbow had no particular shape, the skin hard and white, and something that stuck out like a little pebble. Stroking her arm, she realized she could encircle her biceps with her fingers, and slide them up to her armpit, where they stopped at the unyielding presence of her shoulder bone.

"Sara . . ."

With one fingertip she traced the horizontal line of her clavicle to her throat. Opening her hand she slid it around her neck and then down her back where one, two, three, four, five, six, seven ridges marked the vertical line of her spinal column.

"Remember how it used to be? We used to talk so much, you told me everything."

With both hands, from the almost imperceptible slope of her breasts, Sara counted her ribs and then followed the predictable distance to her hips. The displeasure she felt touching the two promontories marking her pelvis made her keep going. Her knee bone stuck out from the bottom of her skirt—round, obvious, like some mechanical contraption whose simplicity made it ugly.

"If we started talking again it would only be hard at first. Everything is a little hard at first. Come on, open the door, we'll end up laughing, you'll see."

Until she reached her feet, there, so far away, toes too

long, ankles too pronounced, like two roots that had been ripped clumsily from the ground. But this girl staring at her in the mirror, hands where she held hers, hair falling the same way as hers, in the same sweater, the same skirt—"Sara, please . . ."—but hard, as though a century of exhaustion had smacked her in the face, this stupid girl staring stubbornly, her frail eyes, her lips, her nose—"Sara, open the damn door!"—hair falling over her eyes and accentuating her cheekbones, her ridiculous nose—"Sara!"—lay back on the floor, feeling the unyielding parquet beneath each bone, using her forearm as a pillow. Whose steps were those, trailing off down the hall? And those tears, whose were they?

"Eat," her father said.

Sara realized she didn't know how she'd gotten there. They were sitting around the dining room table at her grandparents' house in the country: she, her father, and a woman.

"You're Sandra," Sara said. "You're the woman who's fucking my dad."

Her father slammed his hand down on the table, frightening the woman more than her.

"What do you want," she said more than asked.

"I want you to eat what's on your plate and show a little respect," her father replied.

"It's okay, relax," the woman said, taking his hand, and then turning to look at Sara, giving her a strange smile, as though trying to convey that she understood perfectly.

On Sara's plate lay a cut-up steak and fried potatoes. On the tip of her fork a hunk of meat, skewered. She was supposed to eat it.

"Do me a favor and pick up that fork, right now," her father said in the same tone of contained rage.

"Go on, Sara, have a little," the woman said, slicing off a piece of her own steak and placing it into her mouth by way of example. She was using a faux-natural tone that made her ridiculous, but at the same time seemed determined to be friendly and didn't stop smiling as she chewed. Sara picked up her fork.

"Eat," her father said.

"Don't be so harsh," the woman said.

"I'm not being harsh, I'm doing what her mother should have done a long time ago." And then, to Sara: "Eat, now."

"I'm a vegetarian."

"I could give a shit—vegetarian."

"Please," the woman said.

Sara placed that *thing* into her mouth and began to chew with the awkwardness of someone attempting an unnatural act. Since she didn't feel capable of swallowing, she kept it in her mouth until the dry meat turned into a lumpy mass, inedible, impossible to swallow.

"Swallow," her father said.

Sara struggled, feeling the paste go down her throat.

"Another piece. Now. Come on."

"Let her catch her breath for a second," the woman said.

"Now," her father continued after a short silence.

"I hate you."

It wasn't the silence or the tension of the preceding scene that made the words fall leadenly onto the table. Had she spoken loudly, had she shouted, it would have seemed a childish outburst, but pronounced that way, in a straightforward informational tone, they became mercilessly solid, as though her hatred had surpassed the bounds of passion and taken root in its cruelest realm—that of absolute indifference. Sara had placed her fork down on the plate, taken a sip of water, dried her lips, and said, "I hate you," as though none of the preceding acts outweighed any other in importance, as though each belonged to the same series of banalities.

"I'm not going to eat any more. What are you planning to do about it?"

Nor did this proclamation have the tone expected of a threat, and again Sara's absolute indifference to the repercussions of her decision left her father at a loss. Silence didn't make it any easier.

"I'm leaving, the two of you need to talk," the woman said.

"No, please stay," said her father.

"I think you should talk alone," she replied.

"Go," Sara said in the same unflappable tone.

Her father stood, walked to her, and gave his daughter a resounding slap. The woman rushed over, begged him to stop. She looked like she was about to cry but didn't, instead just kept repeating, "Oh my God," over and over, as though imitating a melodramatic sketch. Sara's father turned to the woman and put his arm around her, trying to calm her. Sara tucked a strand of hair behind her ear and put a hand to her cheek, now burning with her utter indifference. She felt no urge to cry, no shame, no pain. A strange man embracing a strange woman. She wanted to be small, immeasurably tiny, to disappear. She closed her eyes.

"Have you stopped for a second," her father finally said, "for one single second, to think about how much you're making your mother suffer?"

"Have *you* stopped for a second," she echoed, eyes wide, "to think about how much *you're* making my mother suffer?"

They stared at one other without malice, two criminals confessing to the same crime, in mutual understanding. It had been a long time since Sara cared about her role in it all, but for her father the words seemed to reopen an old wound that had never healed properly, his agitation betraying his guilt.

"Get your things," he said, "dinner's over."

They drove in silence for an hour and when they got to the door of her building, Sara's father told the woman to wait in the car, he'd be right down. They didn't look at one another in the elevator. Her father said, "Open the door," and Sara opened the door. Her mother was in the living room watching television. Sara left them there. She heard her father shouting. Heard her mother shouting. Heard her father close the door. Heard her mother turn off the television.

It was February twenty-eighth. Sara weighed 88.6 pounds.

It was a Tuesday, the night she left home, and absurdly warm in Madrid, almost spring-like. She hadn't gone to school all week and her mother, if she'd even noticed, hadn't said a word about it. It was four o'clock in the morning when she walked out of the apartment, trying not to make any noise, taking the stairs. On leaving, she felt dispossessed, like a creature with neither time nor place, and when she opened the door to the street she inhaled deeply, as deep as her lungs would allow, filling them with air. Then she walked to the only conceivable place: the park. The obvious silence of the paths, of the trees, lent the park a strange nocturnal vitality and she felt pleased to be walking there, like someone slowly strolling, reveling, in their own private garden. The lake was still, waiting there, and she sat to contemplate it. When she felt overcome with sleep she stretched out on the grass. Closing her eyes, Sara got the feeling that the ground beneath her body was breathing, that some sort of force— initially almost imperceptible but growing stronger by the second—was holding her to the spot, first sucking her in and then lifting her into the air, weightless, as though she had no body. She stroked the grass without opening her eyes and then clutched it so as not to lose that marvelous feeling, like riding an enormous and immensely powerful horse, clutching the mane of an animal sweeping her along at incredible speed. And Sara began to laugh. It felt as though her joy had spread all the way across the earth and then come and surged up right there in her chest. She felt tears stinging her eyes. She screamed. Screamed to keep from bursting with happiness. Then smiling, overcome, she fainted, or fell asleep.

The owner of one of the sidewalk cafés that bordered the lake roused her, and it seemed to Sara that rarely had she awoken so rested, so jovial as she did that morning. The man, however, was giving her a frightened look.

"You feel okay, kid?"

"Who are you?"

"I'm . . ." And he pointed to the café by the lake but he must have decided it would be absurd to finish the sentence. "Where do you live? Did you sleep here?"

Sara didn't respond, simply stared at the lake and then at the grass on which she'd spent the night. It was cold.

"You feel okay?"

Though concerned, the man was also afraid of something, it was palpable, as was a glimmer of repugnance lurking in the depths of his fear, making him frown.

"Of course I feel okay."

"Where are you parents? Where do you live?"

Sara didn't respond, she just wanted that man to go away, leave her alone, stop talking already so that she could keep gazing at the lake; she wouldn't make any noise, wouldn't bother anyone.

"Kid."

"What?"

"I said where do you live."

"I don't know," she replied just to say something, thinking that this way he might leave sooner, but not only did he not leave he grabbed her wrist and hauled her to the cafeteria, picked up the phone and dialed a number.

"Police, please. Yes, I'll hold."

Hearing that, Sara's blood began to boil.

"Police! Why are you calling the police? What have I done to you?"

"Nothing, not a thing; this way they'll come get you and take you home."

"I don't want to go home."

The man was about to say something but someone must have started talking on the phone.

"Yeah," he said, "listen, I work at the park and this morning . . ."

Sara bit the man's hand so hard she felt her teeth pierce the skin on his thumb. The moment he released her she ran.

"Stop that girl!" he shouted, but the only person who could have done it—a woman crossing the path, who looked to be about forty—almost took a step back, an expression of fear frozen on her face.

Sara veered off the path and headed for the trees, listening to the thud of her shoes, racing as fast as possible. Her mouth was dry and she was running out of breath, inhaling in jagged uneven gulps. She was sure now: she'd have to run away, far, and hide. Her stomach hurt and she felt weak but kept running until a whitish fog told her she was about to faint. Approaching a giant shrub, she climbed in. There was a strong stench of urine and the remains of what must have been an old picnic: some wrappers and an empty cigarette pack. She sat down. No one would see her there. She wiped the cold sweat from her temples with a shirtsleeve. The beating of her heart sounded like heavy banging on a muffled drum. Her saliva had a metallic taste to it. She thought she was going to faint. She lay down.

For an entire hour she feared that the man would find her and force her to go home. She felt it in the sound of each footstep that neared the bush, in each noise that didn't belong to the park itself. Then the fear became hollow and she thought of her mother, of Teresa, of Aunt Eli, but as if they had no texture to them, as if they were simply images stored in her memory, with no repercussions other than that of floating there, weightless. "I left home," she thought, "I ran away," but not even this moved her to sadness or to joy. Everything welled up and then fizzled in that void, where only what was palpable was real or solid: the grass, the wall of leaves formed by the shrubs in which she'd hidden, her hands stroking them, the empty cigarette pack, empty Coke can, the candy wrapper. "They'll come looking for me now," she thought, as if shocked at her indifference, as if wanting to feel shock, "they'll search everywhere for me," but not believing that their images were material enough to do so. Then fear, again, when she heard footsteps and drew her legs up, trying not to make any noise, almost holding her breath. On her pink watch with a minute hand curved like a little worm, an hour went by, and then another, and another, and in each hour her fear grew dense and then hollow, dense and then hollow. And the image of Teresa, and the image of Aunt Eli, and her feet.

Sara looked at her watch at 5:18, because she was thirsty. She hadn't had a drop of water all day, she suddenly realized, despite having felt thirsty the entire time. She decided to give it a little longer because it was still light and people might see her, but even as she made this decision Sara felt her panicky urge for water intensify. She stuck her head out through the twigs and saw a man walking his dog in the distance. This man, too, would grab her by the arm, call the police. She couldn't come out. But she was thirsty. Two feet from the bush was a hosepipe but Sara saw no faucet and was completely parched. She could make a run for it, but didn't know where to run. The water fountain she knew was too far away and there would no doubt be people by the lake. She tore off a handful of leaves and chewed until they formed a little wad. Then she pressed it against the roof of her mouth. After repeating this operation four or five times she ended up swallowing the mass out of sheer anxiety, desperate to quench her thirst. Though the taste was not pleasant, she sensed that it calmed her.

Two hours later it started to grow dusky and an hour after that it was completely dark. And still she waited in the shrubbery, to be absolutely certain no one would see her. When Sara finally stepped onto the path her pink watch said 12:30. Sitting still all day had made her legs numb, and she shivered with the cold, having been motionless for the past few hours, her chest suddenly quivering at irregular intervals. Walking toward the lake, she noted with pleasure that her body was starting to warm up. Lampposts illuminated the deserted path like a catwalk primed for a celebrity expecting a huge audience on the other side of the curtain, except there was no audience, no witness to her joy, no one to pretend for. Sara stepped off the path and walked among the trees. The silence there had a different texture—natural, everyday. It was unreal, imagining that no one had ever walked there before. The moon cast a faint glow on the lake, and the lamps lining the other side were reflected on the water like shards of light. She leaned over and slowly began to drink, calmly, as though for the first time. Satisfied, Sara crossed her legs and inhaled deeply. She wasn't sleepy, she had no memories.

Morning arrived from far off, dawn breaking in one part in the sky and tinting the park with the matte lighting of an old movie. Sara was tired and realized that she had gone all night without moving. There was a sweeper on the other side of the lake. She drank water hurriedly and made for the trees. The light, suddenly, had made shame return, and fear, and though she'd seen only one cleaner and knew that not even he had noticed her presence, Sara felt a cruel stirring of shame at her ugliness. She was disgusting, that's why she had to hide. Her pants had dirt and grass stains on them, and her shirt had a mysterious L-shaped rip that exposed the skin around her ribs. Her hair was dirty too, she realized, as she smoothed a hand through it and her fingers caught in the tangles. She probably smelled bad. This was an almost scandalous realization. She, who had always gone to such lengths not to smell like anything at all, probably now reeked. She couldn't recall the man's face but most certainly remembered the smell of a beggar who'd once approached her close to home, asking for money. That was how she must smell—the same concentrated stench of urine and rot, same sour wine-breath; that must be how people would see her now.

The pink watch with the worm-shaped minute hand said it was 7:30, and Wednesday, but neither of those things was as important as hiding again. With an astonishment bordering panic, she discovered she'd peed in her pants. It must have happened during the night, while she was watching the lake. She hadn't even been aware of it at the time, but now a yellow stain on her light-colored trousers announced the fact like an exclamation of shame.

It was warm that morning and she feared the temperature would bring people out. She hid, as though having planned it, in the same shrub as the day before. She was exhausted and curled up, leaning back, covering herself with leaves so no one could see her. She'd gone almost 30 hours without sleep and when she closed her eyes it felt like everything started to spin. The light didn't bother her, but if she heard a strange sound her eyes flew open and she'd wait, motionless, for the danger to pass. Although it happened repeatedly throughout the morning, Sara was able to rest, dozing but never sleeping, like an animal whose survival depends on constant vigilance. The periods of rest were dark and leaden as caverns and she could feel—oddly aware of each part of her body—the way these or those muscles relaxed while still holding tension elsewhere, as though certain parts segued into others in a concert she herself were unconsciously conducting.

There were no images or voices there. The pleasure she derived from rest (Sara had always loved sleeping in on weekends) was replaced by the obligation to rest, by its necessity. She felt genuine delight at this hardening. No longer feeling guilty for running away from home, no longer thinking of anyone, she allowed herself to be swept off by her fascination at perceiving that she controlled everything down to the last fiber of her own awareness. Every feeling, every bodily sensation was ultimately a controllable fiction. Hunger, the sharp pain in her stomach, disappeared just by thinking about it, by deconstructing it into simple pains until it was nothing but a reaction whose existence was as easy to suppress as wishing it so. The same was true of loneliness. She had only to think about it, to isolate it from other feelings, other reactions, and then watch it slowly dissipate, almost shamefully, like a lie that's been exposed, to return to the state in which she now felt more herself, perhaps, than ever before.

She awoke during the nicest, warmest part of the afternoon. There were voices around her and she made every effort not to move. When they grew distant she sat up, brushing off the leaves she'd used to cover herself. She could see them through the shrub's branches: a group of boys who'd stood, after sitting and talking for a while, and were now ready to leave. Sara both hated and feared them, a single shift in her disposition. They joked and laughed like giants. One of them, as the others walked off, broke from the group and came back toward the bush. He was very good-looking. He wore jeans and had enormous green eyes. She tried not to move but, out of fear, parted the leaves, making a noise which, though in fact very quiet, sounded to her terribly sharp, a dead giveaway.

"What are you doing?" his friends shouted from the distance.

"Looking for my lighter, I think I left it back here," he replied.

Sara was hypnotized by his brawny arms, his shoulders.

"Come on, man!" they shouted.

"Hang on! I put it down somewhere around here, I'm sure . . ." his voice trailed off, almost a whisper. On his knees he searched, patting the grass.

"We're leaving," they yelled.

"Fuck it," he said jumping up, and ran after them.

When night fell Sara emerged from the bush, still thinking about that boy. Not even the lake managed to calm her. She felt danger lurking like a shadow the moment she emerged from her hiding place and took the illuminated path, in the heat of the night, and although not excessive, it lent a special torpor. She didn't turn when she heard noises—first far off, then closer, but stopping, as though wanting to keep a distance—because a strange part of her had accepted fear, as well, had deconstructed it until all that was left was anxiety pursuing her, snapping twigs behind her, taking false steps from time to time. She didn't go sit in the spot she had the other nights because suddenly she decided to face up to it as soon as possible. She waited, standing by the lake, for it to catch up. The noise ceased for a few seconds, perhaps twenty feet away; there was no sign of it for a few minutes. She turned abruptly toward where she thought she'd last heard it and shouted. And slowly the shadow shrank and slunk away when she turned her back to it once more, and Sara knew that it was gone for good because the air became heavy and slow and difficult once more. She walked to the place she liked to sit and contemplate the lake. She drank water, bending over, wetting her entire face. If she'd said, "Move it, get out of here, go jump in the sea," it would have.

Sara awoke in the morning clenching her teeth, again hiding behind the wall of leaves. The pink worm minute-hand of her watch said it was 8:20, Thursday. She clenched them even tighter, for a long time, until her jaw began to ache.

She saw, through the gaps in the branches, that the sky was a steely gray, promising rain. Strong and heavy as that sky, that was how she felt, hard and rough as an animal; it was as though she'd always lived there, behind that wall of leaves, in that shrub, as though the sunlight she'd seen her whole life was the very one now filtering through the branches. And yet the more pleasurable she found the things surrounding her, the more unpleasant her own body among them. Sara grabbed a stick and, rolling up her pants leg, scratched at her thigh until it bled. Then, as though shocked by her own action, she gazed, transfixed, as a fat maroon drop rolled down the whiteness of her skin to the ground, like a flag that's just been invented.

Afternoon was the saddest time of day, and on that one it also rained for thirty minutes, making it worse. She wanted to move but was afraid, again, of being seen. Being taken home was no longer what she feared. Honestly, the thought of going home was something that hadn't really concerned her since the first morning. No, what she feared now was being seen, and her fear, like the air, like the light, altered by the second, swinging from the sort that was tinged with scorn to the hopeless panic that overcame her, soaked and hugging her knees after the rain while straining to hear every little suspicious sound, knowing that she was repugnant and at the same time aware that repugnance was the very key to her hardness, to her control.

It was almost dark when a dog began sniffing at the bush. She realized she must have been staring at this one leaf for a long time. In an attempt to put the cold and the wet out of her mind, she'd resolved to contemplate one of the shrub's branches and then zoomed in until she found her attention focused on a single leaf sticking out at her like a tiny green tongue. First indifferently, then in curiosity, she'd leaned toward it. An hour later, when the dog started sniffing around the bush, Sara was utterly engrossed in its simple beauty. Fleshy-looking, it was divided in two by a vein on its underside that branched off into asymmetrical hands. Water made the other side look unusually dark and shiny. And yet it was not the sum of its parts that made the leaf beautiful, but the fact that it transcended beauty, the leaf did, in a way that made it imposing and indisputable, like a cathedral.

When the dog stuck its snout into the bush and turned its glassy eyes toward her, Sara felt like she'd been caught in a private act. The stupid look on its face lasted a few seconds, the animal mesmerized by her—a strange object. She struck its nose, hard, and it gave a little whimper, followed by two sharp barks.

"Indi!" shouted a woman, calling the animal.

The dog thrust its head in at another spot and stared at her, growling low and throaty; she responded, growling back like a dog whose territory has been threatened.

"Indi!" the voice repeated, coming close. "What is it? Did you find something? Is there a little doggie in there?"

Sara saw two hands part the branches and a rosy

round face appear. She screamed as loud as possible. The woman's face froze in a rictus of panic and Sara ran. There was no one on the path, but fear made her run through the trees. She was panting and felt like her heart was about to explode. The bush she hid in this time was smaller than the previous one so she had to force herself into a narrower space, branches digging into her.

Night fell slowly and Sara didn't dare come out until hours after dark. Upon emerging, she felt that she had quite naturally adopted an animal way of walking, of moving—the cadence of a trot, head slightly forward and down, as though tracking someone's scent. That night she didn't go directly to the lake but first circled it, all the while feeling the authoritative satisfaction of one whose grounds are in perfect order. She wanted to yell, drag herself across the ground, sweat, eat flesh.

Sara would never recall how she got there or what exactly she did that night. She does remember that, waking up in the morning, she was hiding in a bush at the edge of the park. It was a beautiful day and her pink watch said Friday. Her head hurt and her clothes were damp. Her skin, though, was dry and whitish and the feel of wet fabric gave her a visceral displeasure. She took off her shirt and pants and curled up in the beam of sunlight streaming into the bush. Although her body accepted the warmth with pleasure, she remained completely tense.

A man's voice said, "Look, there's no one here."

A woman: "I know."

Through the branches, two bodies lying together on the grass, kissing.

From that moment on, Sara had only extremely vague, disjointed memories of the whole scene: the tips of her shoes, a used syringe, the light, the rotten smell coming from her clothes.

The man was saying, "But there's no one here."

And the woman: "I know."

He parted the woman's legs with his knee and pushed his thigh towards her crotch, licking her neck. Sara felt herself slipping away, as if her senses had reached the limits of the tolerable. Not just the couple but everything, even the most insignificant objects, seemed to be shrieking horrifically, producing a sound that grew exponentially louder until finally it stopped at an unbearably sharp, sustained note.

"No, let's go to your place," she said, but the man kept licking her neck.

It was too hot, or too cold, and the brightness hurt her eyes. The ringing sound was still deafening but at the same time she heard, with perfect definition, the sound of their two bodies rubbing against one another.

"Let's go to your place," the woman repeated, but in an acquiescent tone signaling the opposite, spreading her legs as the man climbed on top of her.

If anyone had asked Sara what she felt, at that moment, she'd say that out of nowhere came a great silence, and then it was as if everything cracked, breaking into individual pieces, and each of those pieces into smaller ones, and so on, until a point that seemed impossible and yet everything still kept breaking into simpler and simpler parts, and that in this process everything not only lost all harmony but stopped making any sense. Sara leapt on the man. Leapt as though destroying him would restore order once more. The woman screamed. Sara can recall her face—her wide-open eyes, her mascara. She bit the man's arm but he threw her off, leaving her sprawled on the grass. It was like challenging a colossus to a fight to the death. She leapt again, trying to bite his neck. Sara remembers the thick heavy air, and that the man finally grabbed her firmly by the shoulders. Meanwhile, she kicked, trying to turn and bite him somewhere, anywhere. She managed to wriggle free and then attacked again. Then nothing.

She must have gotten hit because now, in the room she finds herself in, opening her eyes, Sara discovers that she can't move and feels a sort of pain, a stinging, in her right cheekbone. The room is white, like a hospital. There's a chair by her bed. Lifting her head, she can see her feet, absurdly small, and a door through which she can glimpse a bathroom. A woman walks in. Smiles. Sits in the chair beside her.

"Hello," she says.

"Hello."

"Are you feeling better?"

"Yes," she replies, not knowing why she's being asked that but guessing that the right answer is *yes*. She feels weak.

"What's your name?"

"Sara."

"Someone must be trying to find you; I bet someone's very worried about you, you know." The woman smiles. She's got lipstick on one tooth.

"Can you give me a phone number? Someone we can call and tell you're here?"

Sara recites a number, a name. Both seem to have come from far away, but she remembers them distinctly, simple and decontextualized, like two foreign objects.

"What were you doing in the park, Sara?"

"Nothing."

"Why did you try to hit that man?"

"I don't know."

The woman smiles again.

"You rest," she says, placing a hand on Sara's forehead. "We'll call your mother."

Sara feels the urge to cry. The lipstick-toothed woman gets up and leaves. Then comes a very long and very white silence, a silence inhabited by metallic sounds coming from behind the door and voices off in the distance. A nurse comes in with a little cart, rolls it over to the bed and uncovers it. She says something Sara can't fully make sense of.

"We're not allowed to untie you."

She raises the top of the bed with a lever until Sara is upright with a tray before her on which sit a steaming cup of broth, a little bit of ham and a yogurt. Sara wants the woman to leave but the woman does not leave. She spoons broth into Sara's mouth. One spoonful, then another, and another. The hot liquid burns her guts like acid.

"No more," says Sara.

"You have to eat it all, doctor's orders."

Another spoonful of broth, and another.

"No more, please," Sara says.

"I'm sorry," the bovine nurse replies tenderly.

Sara looks at the ham, feels nauseous and vomits onto the tray. The nurse leans away to avoid being splashed and wordlessly removes the tray and dirty sheet like a dog accustomed to being beaten.

"What did they do to me?" she asks.

"Nothing, sweetheart, what would they do? Try to make you better, that's all."

Sara begins to cry. Slow, heaving sobs. She tries to stop and can't, it's too late. She'd always been so proud of her ability to hold back her tears. Now the shell of her visible strength cracked, it's as if she's melting in the sickening viscosity of snot and tears.

"Poor baby," the nurse says, leaning in with a little cloth she uses to wipe her face and then holds to Sara's nose so she can blow. "Poor, poor baby."

Sara feels contempt for the woman.

Her perfume smell.

Her woebegone eyes.

Her matronly bosom.

But she feels incapable of showing her contempt. Contempt requires too much strength. She's so small, her enemy enormous. This woman could break Sara's bones just by hugging her, could suffocate her with nothing but her body weight.

"I'll talk to the doctor, don't you worry. Cry all you want, nothing wrong with that."

By the time she stops crying, Sara can hardly feel the pudgy hand stroking her hair. The white of the room darkens, turns black, leaden, and later light, and then black again, and in that confusion she is falling into nothingness, a fragile and enfeebled darkness, wanting to be tiny, tinier still: a speck of dust, an invisible insect that can escape under the door, air. But not like before, not feeling the urge to shout but feeling the whole world is on her shoulders and she's going to die, without actually doing it.

"You rest a little," the nurse says, exiting with her little cart.

Then silence. Silence, flooding the room, like a strange part of herself.

It's almost dark out when the door opens and the woman with the lipstick tooth says, without actually entering the room, "Sara? Good, I just wanted to make sure you were awake. Look who's here, look who came to see you."

A woman who looks like her mother walks in, a woman

who, like her mother, wears a blue dress, and a gold chain, and shoes like her mother's, but this woman is also exceedingly pale. And looks thinner, and has purple bags under her eyes. She's also carrying a bouquet of red flowers, which she places on the nightstand, trying to smile. She doesn't know how to behave.

"Sweetheart," she begins.

Sara realizes that now she is supposed to give some sort of explanation—cry, feel guilty; but she can't make any of those feelings show on her face genuinely.

"Does she really have to be tied up like that?" her mother asks, turning to the woman.

"I don't think so, I'll speak to the doctor."

"Good God, look at your eye. Does it hurt?"

Two men come in and free her from a complicated contraption involving straps and buckles. Her mother kisses her. Cries. Sniffles.

"Sweetheart, say something," she says.

Sara doesn't know what to say and says nothing.

"Tomorrow you're going to be moved to another building. They have a program for girls like you. Right, doctor?"

The doctor, a man of about forty wearing a white coat full of pens, whose presence she hadn't noticed until that moment, says, "Yes," and gives a slow, serene nod, a papal nod.

"They're really going to help you, you'll see. You'll be home in a week."

"That depends on her progress," the doctor amends.

"I know. But you will, you'll be back home in a week."

She kisses her again. Sara is sickened by the feel of her mother's tears on her cheek.

"Your father's right outside. Should I tell him to come in?"

"No."

"He asked me to tell you he's sorry. He didn't mean to slap you that day, you know that."

A few seconds later, the doctor kicks everyone out of the room. He holds out a white capsule and a glass of water.

"Take this. It will help you sleep."

It's dark out when the door is closed. A strip of white light shines under on the floor tiles. So many eyes, out there.

It's 10:30 on the worm minute-hand of her pink watch, and Sara is in a different room. She was pushed, in a wheelchair, down an interminable white hall, taken up in an elevator. The only sound the clacking of nurse shoes, the only smell vaguely disinfected. Oral Medicine. Eating Disorders. This room is smaller than the last one, but it does have a window that looks onto what must be a garden. She climbed into a cold bed and a nurse, jabbing a needle into her arm, hooked her up to a transparent tube connected to a saline bag.

"If it gets backed up, if it stops dripping, if the needle falls out, you call me. Try not to move your arm, and don't touch anything," she recited, like the chorus of a song learned by heart. Then another woman walked in.

"You're going to have a roommate," she remarked,

sliding her bed over slightly to make room. "The two of you can chat, that will be nice."

Ana. The door opened and: Ana. The door opened and: Ana's enormous brown eyes and Ana's nose and the mole on her left cheek, and Ana's hands and feet, so like her own, and even a little tube like hers, leading to a contraption attached to her bed that the nurse kept her hand on, as though afraid it might fall.

"Hello," said the nurse.

But Ana said nothing, made no sound to accompany the nurse's words, no movement with her arm. What she did do, throughout the complicated series of maneuvers undertaken to wheel her past, was stare fixedly at Sara the whole time. It was obvious she'd been bathed, even had her hair washed, because Sara was getting a faint shampoo smell. And she had a red hairclip on one side, holding her bangs behind her ear, and a fake-gold ring with a huge lilac-colored stone that looked like a diamond on one finger. And eyes.

"This is going to be nice for the two of you, you'll see," the nurse said. "Ana, this is Sara; Sara, Ana."

They were both about to say *hello* but then didn't say *hello. Hello* would have been what everybody said and they weren't like other girls. They waited for the nurse to leave and then gazed at each other. Both of them wanted to talk, Ana even made a rueful attempt, which foundered, ending in something that sounded like a cough.

"What happened to your eye?" she finally asked.

"I hit a guy."

"Oh."

Ana lowered her gaze slightly, to the sheet. She twisted her ring a few times and then suddenly stared straight at Sara.

"Did you notice we both have names that only have As? Ana, Sara."

She'd launched into the observation almost enthusiastically but halfway through seemed to regret it, and their names, by the time she finished, were spoken almost in a whisper.

"Yeah," Sara replied. "I'm seventeen."

"I'm sixteen."

"You're really pretty."

Ana stared at her gravely when she said that. They remained quiet for a moment.

"That's not true," she said. "I'm not pretty."

"I don't want to be pretty," Sara answered.

"Me either, I don't want to be pretty either," Ana replied hurriedly, as though prettiness excluded her from a group she wanted to belong to.

"I like your mole."

"Thank you."

They fell silent again, continued staring at one another. It wasn't that they had nothing to say, it was that they had too much, and neither of them knew where to begin. Sara would have liked, right off the bat, to tell Ana about the park, the lake, the light of the streetlamps reflected in the water at night. Their age difference had ranked her in a position of superiority, and this had immediately restored her sense of power. Ana had given her a look of admiration when she told her she'd hit that man, and from that moment on Sara had the urge to look in the mirror. She hadn't seen her own reflection in a long time.

"Aren't there any mirrors around here?" she asked.

"In the bathroom, maybe, but you're not allowed to get up," Ana replied.

"Why not?"

"I don't know."

Outwardly, the image of the person in the mirror reflected no evil. She wore a hospital gown with polka dots and had short hair. Though not pale, the girl's skin had a sickly transparency, accentuated by her dark, almost brown, lips. Her right eye, which was totally bruised, looked swollen and had a yellowish tone. Ana's huge, silent brown eyes suddenly appeared behind the girl's back. Like Sara, she'd gotten out of bed and brought her saline bag with her.

"I haven't seen myself in a long time," Sara explained, not moving.

Ana stood, waiting, in the doorway for a moment and then approached, filling the empty section of mirror as though attempting to complete an unfinished portrait, also looking surprised by the girl reflected there.

"I used to look at myself all the time," Ana said. "I looked at myself so much I couldn't stand it, but I couldn't stop, either. Isn't that stupid? I'm so stupid."

"No, you're not stupid," Sara replied firmly, still staring in the mirror, motionless.

Something happened then. Perhaps it was her words. Perhaps it was that Ana had made her comment jokily, but Sara hadn't joked in response. Perhaps it was the soft bathroom lighting and the two of them there, in the mirror, suddenly frozen, as though waiting for someone to snap a photo, as though they'd been instructed not to speak and to stare at one another until there was nothing left to understand.

They were all called together for the first time that afternoon. The oldest girl was nineteen, bleached blonde and named Maite. The next was eighteen and had a horsey smile, which she displayed whenever she didn't know what to do or say, and her name was Nuria. The third in line was also eighteen and had a difficult name that Sara could never remember; she always wore a pair of slippers her mother had brought her. Then came her, and Ana. A woman told them that they were sick and that the first step toward recovery was admitting their illness. Then she talked about fats and their vital function in a woman's body. Finally she explained the rules, which basically came down to a one-hour talk with a psychologist and strict *vigilance*—she emphasized the word—at mealtimes, which could result in their being punished or rewarded, depending. Nobody wanted to talk at first, they all stared at the floor when the woman asked them to introduce themselves. When it was her turn, Sara said her name and that she was seventeen, and had no siblings, and liked to draw, a fact which seemed to really please the woman.

"My mother is a painter; she does portraits—pastels. What do you do?"

Sara felt as if she'd been caught in a lie. She always said she liked to draw because one time, years ago, the teacher had held her drawing up to the whole class as an example. Since then, she'd always said she liked to draw, and that she was going to be an artist, but she'd never truly drawn or painted. What were *pastels*? How could she now say that even though she didn't actually draw, herself, she really liked drawing? Who was going to believe that? Suddenly Sara hated the woman. She, who had felt almost comfortable, who had initially almost accepted Nuria's smile, Maite's hair, the other girl's slippers. Now, inexorably, they became enemies. And it seemed that everyone but Ana was staring at her with that stupid expectant look. It was a clown. The drawing the teacher had held up to the class was of a clown. They were all drawing with crayons and the teacher had walked over to her drawing and fixed it. He'd said, "Look, if you just do this right here . . . See how nice that looks?" and in three quick strokes he'd transformed her anodyne drawing into an incredible clown, a clown that looked like he was smiling but without actually smiling, a clown that looked like he was smiling but sad, and she, for fear of messing it up, hadn't changed a thing. She added some balloons in the background and signed *Sara*, with a line under her name, like Picasso.

"Come on, Sara, tell us. What do you do?"

"I do crayon sketches."

"No *artists* use crayon," Maite said. "They use oil paint, or acrylics, or watercolor. Some people do charcoal sketches. But I've never heard of—"

"Well I use those things, too," she added quickly, "but mainly crayon."

Now everyone knew she was lying. And the teacher had only held up her drawing because he didn't remember he'd actually done it himself.

"Look, everyone, see how good Sara's is?"

And everyone had looked up, amazed, even Teresa had looked amazed, as though silently commending the merit of having kept such a talent hidden, not bragging about it. And it was a lie. A lie.

"So *how* do you sketch with crayon?" Maite wanted to know, refusing to give up.

Sara hated them and hated herself. The thing she especially hated about the whole situation was the feeling of shame, her public humiliation, because it made her weak again, like before, like with Teresa and Luis, and she never wanted to feel like that.

"I use pastel crayons."

"Ha! Pastel crayons. There's no such thing!"

"Of course there is, that's what I use."

"Okay, that's enough now," the woman said.

"But she's lying," Maite insisted, "and *no lying* is the first rule."

"It doesn't matter, I said that's enough."

"I'm not lying, bitch," Sara exclaimed.

"Sara!"

Ana, who'd been playing with her purple ring throughout the conversation, suddenly looked up at her in fear, in admiration, and her regard suddenly made Sara feel invincible.

"If you say I'm lying again, I'll kill you."

"Sara!"

Maite said nothing, and that was a victory. She felt it in Ana's eyes, too, wide open and shiny as a badge of pride.

"Well, let this be an example to all of you. Sara, you're punished: no movie night for four days."

"I don't care."

"Oh, you will. Believe me."

She did care. She cared starting that very night. After dinner—a protracted ritual that took place in silence, under the watchful gaze of two nurses—everyone but her went off to watch the movie, which was always shown in the little room adjoining the cafeteria. Since they weren't allowed to go to the bathroom for an hour after dinner, and even then not allowed to flush, Sara had to sit there listening to them all laugh. Finally, the nurse said she could go to her room. All day long she'd wanted to go to her room, and yet at that moment she'd have preferred to stay.

"Can't I stay here?"

"No. You're punished, you know that."

In the next room everyone was laughing, even Ana. She waited for her in their room, in bed, and stirred lazily when the door finally opened, attempting to feign the torpid irritation of someone who's been asleep for ages. Ana went to her bed and climbed in slowly, trying not to make any noise.

"Was the movie good?" she asked.

"Yeah. Want me to tell you about it?"

"Yes."

Ana recounted the plot quickly, bumblingly, jumping back and forth to explain things she'd forgotten to mention. It wasn't very interesting that way, but Sara was touched and tried to laugh out loud in the places she thought Ana was expecting it.

"I'm not good at explaining movies," she said finally, as though to apologize.

"I think you're good at it," Sara replied.

Her words seemed pondered over, seemed to have come from far away, and she turned toward Ana's bed to speak them. Ana made no reply. Sara could see her silhouette in the light from the park outside; she was lying face-up, staring at the ceiling.

"Maite's a moron. She purposely laughed louder than

anyone at the movie, just for attention. I'm not as brave as you. I was sitting there and I didn't say anything."

"Do you think I lied at group meeting too?"

"No," she answered quickly.

"Thank you."

"They're all morons, aren't they?"

"Yeah."

And she'd have liked to have added: *except us*. They're all morons except us. But she didn't, because Ana turned toward her and they stared at one another in silence. Sara doesn't remember when she fell asleep, when the eyes she was gazing at stopped being Ana's eyes and turned into those other, even bigger eyes that she dreamed of all night, but she contemplated them with the same pleasing emptiness she remembered feeling as she sat before a still round lake, night slipping down like delicate black silk.

Mealtime was the worst. Worse than the one-on-one sessions with the psychologist. Worse, even, than group meeting. As the time drew near the girls inevitably sank into a helpless silence, a silence that meant there were twenty minutes to go, fourteen minutes to go, two minutes to go until the nurse walked into the common room and announced, "Mealtime," knowing full well that there was no place else that those seemingly ordinary words could create an abyss that hovered on the verge of the intolerable. The saline, the meds, the exercise (they were forced to take walks in the morning) inevitably made them hungry, and that made everything worse. It would have been easier, more human, to eat without being hungry. Eating with an appetite seemed not only an unnatural act, but one that—despite their revulsion—they'd been primed for.

They ate hungrily, therefore, violating themselves in the most barbaric and blatant way possible. Silence was simply a way to express solidarity, or something that, like solidarity, was greater than the girls, something that turned them all into a single stomach, a single vanquished will. Sometimes someone cried, but none of them raised their heads from their plates, and then they'd realize that background music had been turned on in order to calm the girls, and the nurse would be humming along to the song; and they'd realize that after the first course would come a second, and then dessert, and they knew they had to eat it all and then sit still for an hour, the others watching a movie, Sara excluded, hoping the nurse wouldn't start some idiotic conversation, feeling each miniscule particle of food making its way through the walls of her stomach, pumping blood, turning to fat; and again the sense of shame, of sliminess, of revulsion pounding in her temples each time the psychologist made Sara talk about her parents—her father in particular—asking her yet again why she'd thrown a rock at that dog, why she'd never called Luis back, why she thought her mother was weak.

Had it not been for Ana, Sara would have been defeated the second afternoon, just as Maite had been, and Nuria, and the girl whose name she could never remember but everyone called Pinkie because of her pink slippers. She, like the others, would have walked in silence from the dining room to the movie, from the movie to a session with the psychologist, from the psychologist to group meeting, silent, hating herself. With Ana it was different. They sat together in the dining room and when one of them thought she couldn't take it anymore the other would move a knee in to touch her, and she would then touch back with her foot; or one would lean into the other, just slightly, until their hips were touching. And that was enough to make things bearable. And this practice involved an element of self-acceptance. Ana one day explained it very well; she said it was like having hair in the land of the bald, and the baldies, out of envy, wanted to shave their heads, after trying to convince them how happy they'd be bald and how unnatural it was to have hair. Sara liked the analogy so much that she told it to Nuria, who used it, as if it was hers, in group meeting. After the customary opening question about how they were feeling, Nuria raised her hand to be first to respond.

"I feel like I'm in the land of the bald, and I have hair," she said, and then, word for word, explained how the baldies were trying to convince her to shave her head.

Ana glanced over at Sara and then the two of them gave Nuria an accusatory look, but rather than take the hint she claimed the whole *land of the bald* thing was a recurring dream she had.

That very night, after Ana told Sara about the movie, they talked for a long time: from that moment on they wouldn't tell anyone anything; it was the two of them, just them two, against all the other girls.

"Like sisters," Ana said.

And she replied:

"No. More than that, more than sisters."

And to underscore their words they stared at one another solemnly, without touching, Ana with the mole on her left cheek and her lilac-colored diamondy ring, she with the almost-faded bruise on her cheekbone and her pink watch with a minute hand shaped like a worm.

"Now we have to take an oath," Sara said.

"What do you mean, an oath?"

"An oath that we'll never be like them."

"Okay."

"I, Sara, swear I'll never be like them."

"I, Ana, swear I'll never be like them."

"When you are weak, I shall be strong," Sara continued slowly, hypnotized by Ana's enormous brown eyes.

"When you are weak, I shall be strong."

"And I will help you."

"And I will help you."

"Always."

"Always."

"Now they can never split us up," Sara said earnestly.

"Never," Ana answered.

And the night was black and rough, like volcanic rock.

Everything changed then, from the slow movie dialogues

in the next room to her conversations with the psychologist. The weakness she'd felt the first few days, the disgust with which she'd observed her body's recovery, they froze. Seeing Ana, hearing her breathe nearby, restored Sara's hardness, the control she'd felt during her week in the park. Two days earlier she'd been on the verge of telling the psychologist what happened there, with the couple making out in the grass; now the memory had been neutralized, shrunk down to almost nothing, she felt she could have suppressed it entirely by sheer force of will.

Ana was weaker. Sara could see that if she wasn't with her, Ana would let herself fall under Maite's sway. Maite, as the oldest, had established a kind of respect-based authority, evidenced by the fact that no one questioned her word and by her preeminent spot at the dining room table. If Sara hated Maite, however, it was not for her authority but for her control over Ana, at times when Sara could not be there for her.

"Maite says you lie more than you speak," Ana told her the night after they'd taken their oath, getting ready to go to dinner.

"Do you believe that?"

"No," she replied, but to Sara it seemed, from Ana's tone, that she wasn't telling her everything. Something in the fragile structure of those brown eyes, which Sara thought about tirelessly, had collapsed, or was on the verge of collapse.

They sat down, like always, without looking at one

another, in the same spots they'd occupied since their first meal. It was an important day: dinner officially marked the end of Sara's punishment; after the meal she'd be allowed to watch the movie with everyone else. She'd been thinking about it all afternoon, and this had kept her in high spirits until Ana told her what Maite had said. They were serving vegetables, fish, and mashed potatoes for dinner.

The meal—like all meals—followed to the letter the ritual adopted from the start. No one looked up from their place but everyone was perfectly aware of the state of everyone else's tray. No one ate faster or slower than anyone else. If one girl seemed to get slightly ahead of the others, she'd linger over something else so as not to finish first. None of them spoke to the others. If they needed anything they asked the nurse directly.

Sara broke the rules that night. Walking in she'd almost bumped into Maite and had given her a look of provocation. Sara's rage focused on Maite's bleached blonde hair, the tone of her voice, her hands. Then it fell to her plate. Maite hadn't touched her mashed potatoes.

"I'm not eating the mashed potatoes," Maite said aloud, when everyone else was already almost finished.

"Yes, you are," the nurse replied matter-of-factly, giving it no importance.

"I've never eaten them. I never ate them at home. My mother always said I didn't have to."

"My mother always said I didn't have to," Sara mimicked.

It was as though a bomb of silence had been dropped onto the table. Maite shot her a look of hatred.

"Sara!" the nurse barked.

The others glanced up from their plates like a herd of does waiting for two bucks to fight.

"I'll throw up if I eat them," Maite said to the nurse, evading Sara's challenge.

"No, you won't. Because you know that if you throw up you get a double portion."

"But that's not fair," Maite replied.

"What wouldn't be fair," the nurse explained, patient as Solomon, "is if you didn't have to eat them when all the other girls have to eat things they don't like all the time. You know the rules: if you're not allergic, no excuses."

Sara felt Ana's foot on her own like an acknowledgment of her worth. She could almost feel herself stroke Ana's cheek with her eyes. Ana had chosen her, chosen Sara, and the touch of that tiny foot on her own—gentle at first, then with increasing pressure—was confirmation of that. Sara felt invincible.

"I'll throw up if I eat them," Maite repeated, very quietly, as though talking to herself.

"Hey, Maite!" Sara shouted. "Maite, watch this!"

She scooped up some mashed potato with one hand and crammed it into her mouth like an animal. Maite's face froze in revulsion.

"Sara!" the nurse yelled.

"Look!" she said, taking what was left on her plate and

smearing it all over her face. Maite vomited onto her tray, and Sara was pulled by the arm from the dining room.

"This means no movie night for a week."

"I'll be out of here in a week."

"Not at the rate you're going, young lady," the nurse replied, locking her into her room.

The afternoon looked warm and red in the small park below the window, but it wasn't the same without Ana; without Ana there to sit calmly and contemplate it with, she felt even more restless at the trees' deep reds and oranges. She was on edge. She wanted to break something, to scream. By the time Ana returned, she'd calmed down.

"How was the movie?"

"Pfff, I'd already seen it. It was a cowboy movie."

"I don't like cowboy movies."

"Me neither."

Not mentioning what had happened at dinner was the ultimate demonstration of Ana's idolatry.

"Want me to tell you what happened the week before I was brought here?"

"Yes."

Ana still didn't know, although Sara had made reference to her days in the park. From the start, she'd wanted the moment she told Ana to be just like this: nighttime, silent, no chance of interruption. She spoke slowly, almost in a whisper, describing every detail as best she could. At some points she felt Ana wasn't getting it, felt like she was doing a bad job, and said, "Wait, that's not right," over and over, or, "I can't explain it." In others, as though someone were dictating to her what to say, she felt her words could be smelled, and touched, her words were the leaves themselves, and the lake, and the night settling in over the trees. Ana, though she looked directly at Sara for a few minutes, then turned her head to the window, the mole-side of her face to Sara. In that position, Sara sensed her words making an obvious and profound impression on Ana, fingers twisting the lilac-colored diamondy ring, eyes looking at the park, at something that, while not the park, lay beyond it, farther away, or deeper inside perhaps.

The next day at breakfast they were told that their families were coming to visit that afternoon, and they would be given half an hour, after lunch, to get ready. Clothes. All the girls started talking about how much they missed their clothes. Sara, from the start, had found the uniform anonymity of their hospital gowns comforting, but she saw the way Ana's eyes lit up thinking about putting on her own pants, her blue sweater. Sara was given a pair of pants and a green shirt that her mother must have brought from home.

When Ana emerged from the bathroom, in her own clothes, Sara lurched quickly into sadness. She looked like she was ready to go. Like she was about to leave—with that sweater and that hairpin and those patent leather shoes and that mole on her cheek—and never come back.

"How do I look?"

"Very pretty," Sara replied.

"Are you looking forward to seeing your parents?"

"No, are you?"

"I don't know," Ana said. "A little, I guess."

"I want my parents to die."

"Me, too."

"Then why did you just say you were looking forward to seeing them?"

"A little, I said I was looking forward to it a little."

"I'm not looking forward to it even a little. What I want is for everyone to leave us alone and the two of us to go to a park and hide all day and come out at night."

Those words, or perhaps Ana's memory of Sara's words the night before, brought an almost unconscious smile to Ana's lips.

"Yeah," she said.

"And for our fathers, and mothers, and the nurses, to die."

"Yeah."

"Can you imagine? The two of us, not eating anything, no one telling us we have to, just sitting by the lake."

"Do you really think we could do that?" Ana asked with a hint of incredulity. "You know the doctors won't let us see each other after we're released."

"Yes, but we're going to run away."

"We can't," said Ana, very somber.

"No, not from here, from home. When we get sent home we'll run away and meet at the lake, at night." And Ana's silence was the most profound and solemn way of saying *yes*.

They each had a half-hour with their parents and after that came a group session with all of the families. Sara's parents were waiting in the second room. Everything about the visit was slow and difficult. Her mother couldn't stop wringing her hands; her father was wearing a tie. Her mother had never wrung her hands; her father hated ties. It was cold in the room. Her mother did most of the talking; her father said almost nothing; she herself spoke not a word.

"This is ridiculous," her father said finally, almost angry. Her mother said a few more things. Sara doesn't remember the words, she remembers the smell of cologne, her father's stomach, his shirt; she remembers the floor lamp and the hospital armchairs. Before the half-hour was up, her mother said:

"Oh, look who else came to see you!"

The door opened, and there was Teresa.

"Sara," she said.

Sara felt as though they'd laid a trap for her. Surrounded, she was surrounded. A moment longer and she'd have said *hello*, but she remained silent, awaiting Teresa's next move, which was simply to repeat her name.

"Sara, it's Teresa," her mother said.

"I don't know you."

"I don't believe this," said her father.

Teresa started to say something but gave up in the end, as though she'd realized that this Sara—the one there now—was, in her own way, rebelling against the Sara who'd borne Teresa's indifference over the phone, and it seemed somehow justified. Not acknowledging her was a way of quashing that feeling of defeat and becoming unassailable once more, hands on hips, there, in that little hospital room, despite the resolute corporeality of her friend.

"Sara," Teresa said for the last time, changing her tone, making clear that she knew what her friend was doing, and that it had gone far enough.

"I don't know you. I don't know who you are."

Teresa's chin quivered pathetically.

"Leave."

Teresa rushed from the room.

"Daughter," her father remarked in amazement, as though having just made a discovery, "you are not only sick, you're cruel."

"Please," her mother said.

"Did you not just see what I saw?"

"Please."

The group session didn't change anything, despite the psychologist showering praise on anyone willing to offer a comment. The few who did speak adopted a sort of the-atrical affectation, almost unconsciously, which shot their credibility; meanwhile, for the entire hour, Sara thought of nothing but Ana's hands. Once all the parents had left, the girls sank into a crestfallen but relaxed silence, like that of someone who finally closes a door and no longer has to pretend, and almost out of convenience adopts a look of contempt.

Ana was very serious, staring at her from the other side

of the common room. Sara could have gone to her, could have told her, say, about Teresa having showed up. But she didn't, because suddenly she had the feeling that Ana's mind was engaged in a raging battle with itself. Ana had never looked at her like that before, eyes half-closed. Anyone seeing her for the first time would have been convinced it was a look of hatred. She'd adopted that look the moment her parents left, that solemnity, and Sara got the sense that Ana was actually forcing herself to the limits of contempt.

What's more, she felt the roles they'd been playing since she stopped eating had been inverted: now Sara was the object of observation, the one being analyzed with the same severity that she herself once employed. Round and leaden came Ana's look from the other side of the room. There were voices murmuring and shadows moving, and everything, even the apparent ambiguity of the environment, seemed predisposed toward contempt.

This was replaced by a strange complacency. Despite neither of them abandoning her expression of disgust, the air grew sweeter. Sara was sure of this when Ana seemed to offer a tiny smile. If asked to explain it, Sara couldn't have articulated her joy. She might, perhaps, have said it was like a pain that subsides without disappearing, a pain that is suddenly justified and by virtue of its justification nearly vanishes. And then she gave Ana the same look, to seal the act of love. Never before had Sara realized that she lived inside another person. It was as if, though neither of them stopped looking at the other, the silence had swapped their bodies and now, from the other's perspective, they were slowly destroying *themselves*. The same act was now being undertaken from the body of the other, with more intensity, more force. Sara stood and went to Ana.

"Come, Ana, let's go to our room," she said.

Sara walked behind her without knowing what they were going to do, what they'd say once there, and as she walked, gazing at Ana's back, her buttocks, her feet, she was overcome with fascination for Ana's tiny, fragile-seeming body, still dressed in the street clothes her family had brought, short hair pulled back behind her ear with that hairpin. It was the same fascination she'd felt the first day, when she saw her being wheeled in on her cot, but now pulsing in her throat like a contraction, rising all the way from her feet. When she closed the door she had no idea what she was going to say, what might happen. Ana's breasts, beneath her blue sweater, looked bigger than they did in the hospital gown.

"We have to see each other naked," Ana said, still serious, a hint of solemnity to her voice. Sara felt her stomach contract quickly.

"Now?"

"Now."

They'd never seen each other naked before. Part of the ritual that made them unusual was their awareness of how ugly their naked bodies were. Up until that moment, without ever having discussed it, they'd used the bathroom one after the other to change. If one closed the door, the

other didn't dare enter, or even knock, and this increased
the solemnity of being naked, a private act so unpleasant
that it could never be contemplated. But now Ana had said
they had to see each other naked; Ana, who never said anything, had said that they had to see each other naked and
the words had inexplicably soothed Sara's throat and at the
same time shot down to her stomach in a quick palpitation.
Ana took off her sweater. Sara her shirt.

"Wait a second," Sara said, and went to pull the blinds
halfway so no one could see. The room drained of light, taking on a gentle, almost matte penumbra. They took off their
pants at the same time, and their panties, and their socks.
Now they were naked. Ana dropped her arms to her sides;
she did too. Ana's breasts had a round, asymmetrical simplicity to them and her nipples looked almost like a smudge,
the color so close to that of her skin. Her pubic hair was
bushy and black and Sara was hypnotized by it, as though
it were a sign of fragility, something that might cause Ana's
whole body to shatter. She felt Ana's eyes on her, doing the
same thing —loving her and destroying her at once, pausing mercilessly at the spindliness of her legs, lingering on
her crotch, climbing her ribs—and wanted to leap on her,
scratch her, bite her face; but no, they had to stand there,
the two of them, a few feet apart, like pillars of salt, eyes
flicking up and down, devouring one another.

Ana stepped toward her and held out a hand, as if to
touch Sara's breast.

"No," Sara said, and Ana's hand froze and then she

looked into her eyes for the first time. "We can't touch," Sara finished.

"Of course," Ana replied slowly, as though this had been the one thing left to understand. "Now we have no secrets."

Nuria left that day. When it was announced in the dining room, everyone looked at her as though it were impossible that she, the girl no one had even really noticed up until then, was actually going to be the first to go.

"What do you mean you're leaving," asked Maite, whose authority had been undermined since the incident at dinner.

"You heard," the nurse remarked, "she's leaving, and if the rest of you follow her example you'll be able to go home soon, too."

Nuria had been an invisible presence up until that day. She spoke, but never too loud or with too much conviction. She ate, but never finished first. She was, ultimately, substitutable.

All of the girls, with the exception of Ana and Sara, seemed to take the nurse's advice quickly, intuitively, because starting that very afternoon they fell into emulating Nuria's invisibility. No one wanted to speak, or eat, or laugh more than anyone else. But silence, too, was dangerous; silence betrayed them. What happened next was rather like life: their performance, at first self-conscious, over the course of the day took on the routine nature of something automatic, and in their sessions, perhaps without even realizing it, they began to describe themselves not as they were but as they pretended and, perhaps, really believed themselves to be.

For Sara, accompanying Ana to their room became a reprieve from that increasingly irritating situation. They took off their clothes, like the first time, but now with no need for words. Sara would give her a look, or Ana would motion with her eyes, and the pair of them would head to their room. Silent, naked, standing closer each time, on the verge of touching though without ever doing it, the smell of Ana's body rising up in a mix of soap and shampoo, Sara's feet cold on the floor tiles, the metallic sound of carts being wheeled past the door. All of it precise, all of it repeated in the same slow ritual, the rules created as they went.

It was raining desperately that afternoon. It had been two days since Nuria left and each girl was anxiously awaiting her turn, as though every gesture, every expression could be the one to finally save them. Sara, although immersed in her fascination for Ana, saw that Maite's rancor was starting to eat away at her. At meetings she deliberately tried to provoke Sara, questioned whatever she said. In the face of that open confrontation, Sara reacted—thanks to Ana—with silence and indifference, irritating Maite even more. That afternoon, warm and humid—suffocating—after the rain, the four remaining girls sat in the common room, not speaking but restless to the point of hysteria.

Sara and Ana went to their room, a decision made almost without glancing at one another, like old lovers who anticipated everything, down to the other's desire. When they were naked, the door opened and there in the threshold were Maite's feline eyes, her bleached blonde hair.

"Ha!" she shouted. "I see you!"

Sara turned to look at Ana and saw that she was ashamed, covering her breasts with her hands.

"I hate her so much," she whispered.

They dressed quickly, and when they were at the door ready to walk out, the psychologist appeared.

"Ana," she said, "come with me, let's have a little chat."

Ana turned quickly to Sara, as though desperate for help.

"Don't worry," Sara replied, "I'll see you at dinner."

"Okay," Ana responded, the concern on her cheeks softening slightly. Sara stood there in the doorway, watching them walk down the hall: the psychologist in her white coat, clogs clunking; Ana in her hospital gown, diminutive and silent, her small hands hanging by her asexual hips, her almost boy-like hips, walking down the hall toward the office door, which the psychologist unlocked and then opened, waiting for Ana to enter first.

"After you," Sara heard the woman say.

Ana turned back, before walking in—enormous brown eyes, for the last time, looking at her.

Sara realized she'd left that very night, when Ana didn't show up at dinner; this was confirmed upon returning to the room to find all of Ana's things gone. She didn't go to bed for quite some time. It would have been impossible to sleep when even the walls retained Ana's smell, when even the air retained her presence—gazing at her from the bed overlooking the park. When she finally tried to go to sleep, it was only to keep from becoming even sadder. Under her pillow she found Ana's lilac-colored diamondy ring. She put it on.

Maite left. Then Rosi. One day she was moved to a new room. A woman who looked like her mother came to visit and told her that she loved and missed her. That was before she was taken into the same common room and the same doctor repeated the same words about the importance of fats in a woman's body. And before she was introduced to five new girls whose names she refused to learn. She said that her name was Sara and that she liked to draw. They asked what kind of drawing. She said pastel crayon. No one commented on that. It was hot. She must have said something mean at dinner because the nurse punished her: no movie night. She said she didn't care. It was true.

She had once wanted so badly to get out of there. Now she wanted nothing. If anyone had asked, she wouldn't have said she was unhappy. Every day was the same, repeated over and over; there was no pain, though neither was there grace. The psychologist asked her to talk about her father and she did, like someone inventing the storyline of a novel they were supposed to have read.

That batch of girls left and others arrived and told her

their names. The same doctor repeated the same words about the importance of fats in a woman's body. She said that her name was Sara and that she liked to draw. No one asked a thing. A woman who looked like her mother brought flowers and said she missed her but there was no conviction behind the words. Sometimes, in the afternoons, she'd look out the window of the common room and breathe deeply while looking down at the park. She no longer wanted to be in it. It must have been summer.

More girls came and said their names. She watched them come and then go just as the light came and then went through her bedroom windows, just as the nurses came and then went in their small timid, almost sweet whiteness, just as Ana came and then went. The first few days after her departure she'd missed Ana a lot, so much that Sara actually believed that her own strength had depended on Ana and she'd be unable to regain it until she saw her again. She continually evoked her memory so as not to forget a single gesture, a single conversation, and every time the psychologist summoned her she imagined that it was to tell her that Ana had run away from home and that she, as her best friend, must know where she'd gone. She imagined all of the doctors physically torturing her, asking her about Ana, making her bleed, and her, in the center of it all, lips sealed, quiet as death, not telling them that Ana was waiting for her by the lake. But none of that happened, just as Ana didn't come visit, not even once.

At first she felt betrayed, but she kept giving her second chances. She'd think, for example, "I'll give her until Wednesday, and if I don't hear anything by Wednesday, then I never want to hear from her again." But Wednesday would come and she'd give her another chance, conjuring up the most unlikely of circumstances that might have befallen her friend.

When a month had gone by, she felt incapable of keeping up the farce and, after a few days during which hatred was still too much like love, she began trying to convince herself of how little she cared. Ana, however, was still in too many places: in the dining room, gazing at her from the other side of the common room, naked standing before her like a pillar of salt, one that now was indeed forever immovable.

One Friday, when they were about to have lunch, she suddenly realized that she hadn't thought of Ana all day, and this made her feel better. One day she had trouble remembering her hands. Another day she threw the ring into the toilet.

More girls arrived. One of them looked like Ana. She, too, had small feet and almond-shaped eyes that were the same shade of brown, shiny and hard. Sara told the girl her name was Sara and that she'd like to learn to draw.

"You don't know how?"

"Not very well."

"I can teach you, if you want."

She would never remember the girl's name, but Sara's memory of the afternoon light, as the two of them sat at a table in the common room, was clear.

"What would you like to draw?"

"Clowns," she replied. And then she learned (it wasn't actually that hard) to draw funny clowns that hardly took more than four circles and two exes for eyes, and clowns sitting on top of balls, and even clowns like the ones her teacher had drawn that you couldn't tell if they were happy or sad, or thin or fat, just as she couldn't tell if she was thin or fat, and she felt the shrinking memory of Ana, who now had no voice because she couldn't recall her voice though she remembered her words, and through all of this Sara was searching for the *thread*, which is what the psychologist had said she needed to find; it wasn't actually a thread, of course, but was similar, she said, to a thread—a place where something went wrong, a memory that couldn't be explained—something that she could begin to tug at in order to unravel the tangled mess inside her, because she was all tangled up inside and what it felt like was a deluge of words, of specific words, words like *Ana*, like *you're very pretty*, like *when you are weak, I shall be strong*; but not like before when she felt blood pumping down to her stomach in quick, nervous palpitations, now it was like she felt ashamed of some part of the girl she'd been when she said those things, ashamed not of the words themselves but of herself actually pronouncing them, because the truth was—and it was a very difficult truth—that without having opened her mouth, without

speaking during group session, after that girl had taught her
to draw clowns something inside her cracked, and it was
something shaped like words that, though not yet spoken,
gushed forth from long ago, from when she was seven years
old and Teresa's mother died of a heart attack and she had
to go a week without seeing her and didn't know how to
react when she finally saw her at school again, all pale, and
wanted to say nice things and tell her how sorry she was but
instead she suddenly hardened, annoyed by Teresa's weakness, and stuck out her tongue; and that same hardness now
dissolved into the words that brought her back to Ana—her
black pubic hair and her feet and the mole on her cheek—as
the doctor repeated the same words about the importance
of fats in a woman's body and she herself repeated, and understood, and accepted that the words were true, though
with the same gag of disgust in her throat when she looked
at herself in the mirror, all soft and naked—her tiny breasts
and tiny buttocks and tiny legs—and she wanted to vomit
at the sight of her soft blubbery body, inarticulate, which
is why she said that afternoon at her session with the psychologist that she felt revolted, and the psychologist asked
her why and she said she didn't know, and the psychologist
asked again, and she said she didn't know and the psychologist insisted that she did know, all serious, almost shouting, and then suddenly up cropped Luis and his tongue as
he kissed her the afternoon of Teresa's birthday, and the
slimy disgust of the pool, and the letter opener and that dog
she saw at her grandparents' house and her father, all of

it spewing from her mouth like vomit, gushing forth, hot
words pouring from her lips, and the psychologist asking,
"What else?" and her saying there was nothing else, and the
psychologist repeating, "What else?" and it was as though
her authoritarian manner served to barge like a fury into the
vault of Sara's memory, the memory reserved for the park,
for the lake, the things that had hardened into a cyst that she
couldn't talk about though the psychologist said, "Of course
you can," but it was like a very hard cyst—and then time
was slowing down once more, and there was silence, not the
absence of sound but absolute silence, shattering things into
little pieces, smaller and smaller pieces that made less and
less sense, that man licking the woman's neck on the grass
in the park and her wanting to destroy it all, to destroy the
man, the woman, the unbearable touching of their bodies,
the woman's open legs and the unarticulated reprieve from
that grotesque, ugly pleasure that was ruining the softness of
the leaves, ruining the color of the sky and her thinness, her
ugliness was why she leapt on him, to put an end to it, not
in order to destroy it but in order to be destroyed, the same
way that something had destroyed the man who drowned in
the lake all those years ago, the man with his USA T-shirt
and one bare foot, the other still wearing a shoe, the same
way something must have destroyed him and left him—ugly
and beautiful at the same time—floating in the lake's still
waters, forever indecipherable, a clown both laughing and
crying at the same time, and that is why she, too, began to
cry. And when the psychologist held her and slowly stroked

her hair, she thought of something farther away still, and harder still. "Is that why you made Ana undress for you?" "What?" "That's why you made Ana undress in front of you, isn't it, Sara? I know what happened, I talked to her the last time and she told me that you made her," "What do you know?" "Everything. That's why you did it, isn't it?" and then the world went stock-still, like a frozen image in a film: Ana, and Ana's little feet and her hands and the mole on her left cheek, and the asymmetrical beauty of her breasts and her eyes, especially her hard eyes when they looked at each other in the mirror on the first day, dissolving now into something else, something like light; "You can tell me; that's why you made her do it, isn't it, Sara?" and it was so easy to say "Yes" because saying yes was saying *You're very pretty* and saying *When you are weak, I shall be strong*, and more than anything it was saying, *I don't love you anymore*, but now without the memory of Ana's hands causing pain, Ana's hands in her memory now calm and still, like the yearning felt for an impossible lake.

MARATHON

HE LIKED RUNNING the way a little kid likes gazing up at the sky—irrationally, with no thought of stopping. He'd always liked it, and couldn't imagine that he might one day stop, just as he couldn't imagine that anyone might stop being someone's brother or sister, or one day change mothers. Running was the most intimate of acts, a realm not even Diana or his university friends could enter, and yet it was one of his few absolute essentials. Twice a week, three times if possible, he performed the slow ritual of the running shoes, the T-shirt, with the confidence of someone effortlessly coaxing pleasure from an old lover at precisely the right moment. And for the past three months—the time since the wedding—it had held even greater appeal, because now the park closest to home was far bigger, and thus offered a greater variety of possible routes. He discovered this with the excitement of a child playing for the first time with a long-coveted toy and holding back, as though to draw out the pleasure of the encounter, savor it to the point of exhaustion.

Diana didn't understand, or if she did, she hated it now that they were married. The week after their wedding she'd tried insisting several times that he let her go with him, and though he tried every excuse to dissuade her (she'd get too tired, she'd hate it, she'd complain the whole time) there came an evening when finally he had to give in. It was, from the start, as if he were against Diana entering this realm, as if he wanted it for himself alone. He knowingly took her on the hardest route and made zero effort to adapt to her pace. After ten minutes she asked him to slow down. After fifteen she gave up and went home. And although pleased by the effort she'd made (it was patently obvious, and therefore flattering, that Diana had pushed herself to the limit in her attempt to keep up with him), he was put off by her weakness, her lack of stamina. Plus, why was Diana so set, now that they were married, on taking part in things she'd shown no interest in over the course of their eight-year courtship? That day, he felt justified in his one-time resolution never to marry, even regretted having done it, having capitulated to Diana's family and their concerns.

"You did that on purpose," she said when he got back, an hour later.

"Did what?"

"Tried to wear me out, you did it on purpose."

"I did not," he lied. Diana was being ridiculous, and looked ugly, which she perhaps never had until that moment. Though she'd already showered and had been home for a while, resting, her cheeks were still flushed from the effort. Her breasts looked too small, or too insubstantial some-how—a part of Diana that hadn't changed now struck him not as unpleasant but insipid, utterly lacking in appeal. The fact that her breasts, of all things, were the focal point of his disgust left him confused, because he'd often thought they were one of the sweetest, loveliest parts of her body.

"I know you too well," she insisted. "You did it to tire me out, at least have the balls to admit it."

"Think what you want, but it's not true."

He walked into the bathroom to shower and locked the door. He'd never locked the bathroom door on Diana before but he did it then, because suddenly the possibility of her coming in as he was washing up bothered him. And though she didn't try, he still felt safer this way, and also pleased with himself for making it clear that his runs belonged to an altogether private realm. There was no reason for this to be a problem, he thought, no reason for her to get upset; all couples, no matter how happy, need their own breathing space. Accepting as much wasn't an admission of defeat, it was just reality. That's what he told her, speaking the words in the same tone in which he'd thought them in the shower, and at first, judging by Diana's expression as she listened, he thought that deep down she got it, and knew that he was right. She did not, however, stay up with him to watch the movie being shown on TV that night. She said her head was killing her and that she wanted to go to bed.

A translator. She was a translator. Not like him, with an active job in probate law at a local firm, but a translator. If at least she did literary translation—short stories or poems—

maybe her life would be saved from absurdity, but Diana's translations were almost always industrial machinery manuals, kitchen appliance instructions, directions for the assembly of tents. How could anyone be happy with that? It was odd, actually, that he'd never thought about it until now. Seeing her asleep in bed when he left in the morning, phoning at lunch to discover that she wasn't even up yet, coming home after work to find her at the computer was starting to give him the impression that she was part of the furniture— her long black hair, slippers, thrown-together outfits worn for comfort—and there was this feeling that sometimes rose up in his throat, strangling him, something like tedium.

They'd known each other for eight years, but maybe they didn't know each other. At first he'd liked Diana's almost undetectable vulnerability, her eyes. They kissed two weeks after meeting and made love for the first time a month after that, in a hostel room whose cost they split, a room whose dinginess struck him as a bit sad when she confessed, afterward, that she'd been a virgin.

"I didn't tell you because I didn't want to scare you off, and because I wanted you to be the one," Diana had said, and he didn't know whether to hold her or scream, to say he loved her or grab his clothes and run.

"I love you," he said.

Their first three years were like those of so many other couples who'd recently graduated from university. They shared the same group of friends, they had parties to attend. Every summer they went to the beach (she liked the south) and at Christmas, maybe skiing. They were reasonably happy, a garden-variety sort of happy—no tragedies, no drama. Sometimes, stopped in the car at a red light, they kissed; they held hands at dinners. Sometimes they were used as the example of a perfect couple.

The fourth year, Diana went to England to teach Spanish. He told her (they'd argued a lot, in the preceding months) that they'd probably break up then, she shouldn't even think of it as tragic, she would probably meet someone else and so would he. But they kept calling each other. For a few months, he dated a girl named Marina whose haircut reminded him of Diana and who he eventually broke up with, out of sheer boredom. Diana wrote him long letters that said absolutely nothing and yet served as a reminder of her uncomplicated presence, of the near-certainty that this woman's entire life was devoted to his happiness. When she returned, he went to pick her up at the airport, and they kissed like it was the first time.

"I love you," Diana said, and he thought then that it would be unfair to ask for anything more of life.

The years following seemed like a slow, inexorable road to matrimony. He saw them differently now, though he realized how valuable Diana's presence had been at that time. He'd begun working in the probate division at the law firm and found it hard not to lose his sense of humor after long sessions in which, too often for his liking, he had to keep relatives of the deceased from tearing each other to shreds.

It was, with rare exception, as though death brought out the worst in people, reduced them to settling affairs in the most vicious of ways. Telling Diana stories after work provided such relief that she became necessary for his survival, because no matter how often he did, she always wore an expression of utter shock, of incredulity, and her incredulity served not to absolve the others but to save him, placing him in a higher order than the one in which he was forced to live.

Two months after she got her translator job they married. He'd always found weddings a bit sad, and his own was no exception.

"This is just a formality," he'd told Diana three days before the ceremony, but in truth her dress weighed on him like a white death. It wasn't a formality, or a costly performance that entailed the banqueting of people they—more or less—cared about, but love, crashing into his awareness like some terrible white elephant in the form of a wedding dress, a balding man who claimed to represent God, Diana's mother smiling for the camera, Diana's friends saying, "She's a first-class product, so you better make it last" and making other jokes, all of them drunk on his dime ("Throw the flowers already, Diana!"), the altar boy dressed in white, the priest dressed in white, Diana's brother in that horrible white hat, and him, there, in the middle of it all, pretending not to be on edge. He asked Diana if they could leave after the cake, because to stay any longer would have meant throwing in the towel, declaring defeat in the face of a ritual of forced happiness, saying yes to his mother, who sometimes couldn't conceal the sadness that living alone was going to bring her and quickly wiped away a tear so her mascara wouldn't run, saying yes to the waiters already handing out cigars and matchboxes unoriginally personalized with their names, yes to pictures ("A little more, right there; now put your arm around your wife!"), to the guests. When they got to the apartment—which back then was almost devoid of furniture—they made love in the least fearful and wretched way they could, and he thought he understood why Diana sometimes froze when on the verge of being naked: because she was afraid, blinded by the responsibility, because her body, a woman's body (like a marathon route disappearing in the distance) was sometimes a frightening panorama to contemplate.

Running was the great liberation. Particularly in the days following the wedding because not only was it an escape from Diana's presence, which suddenly irritated him, but also from his own mood swings. If anyone had asked, he wouldn't have known how to articulate what it was he thought about on his runs. More than the technical aspects of his exertion (how much energy to conserve for the steepest inclines, when to do his sprints, whether he could keep from hitting the wall at twenty miles), the act of running was inward, self-contained, its own erotic world of perfectly conditioned machinery. He might have said, for instance, that nobody who doesn't run could understand the satisfaction of controlling one's own fatigue, or that there were moments in which he didn't feel his body belonged to him in the same way as other people did (so much a part of them that they could never see themselves as separate from it) but instead felt as if he took leave of it, as if he were aware of each of his muscles, controlled each one absolutely and yet did so from elsewhere, somehow, as though only in the act of running did his body stop being him and became something he possessed.

The park had a life of its own, too, and he formed a part of it. A life silently established in the invisible relationships between all the runners. Like a spider's web, it skipped from one to the next, in the form of jealousies, provocations, challenges, propositions; measuring up the next guy was not simply a matter of inspection, it was knowing whether you could beat him without having to run alongside him, it was passing him on the steepest incline without letting the tiniest bit of effort show on your face and then perhaps waiting for him to catch up so you could do it again; it was comparing running shoes, legs, sweat, all without ever letting it be noticed, without speaking it.

He might not have seen the guy in a green T-shirt the very first day, but once he started following him it was as if the guy had been there all along. And he realized, almost with pleasure, that *he* was the only person who could outpace him. This man was thinner and had an asymmetrical rough-hewn beauty about him, even in the way he ran, pumping his arms too high in the stride, and seemed oblivious to his presence. More than a thin, redheaded runner, he was part of the park made visible, and mobile, something whose life didn't extend beyond the trees, which is why when they first met (he turned out to work at the greengrocer's next to his house) it took a minute to recognize him.

"You run, don't you?" the man said, grabbing the bunch of asparagus he'd asked for. "I've seen you lots of times, in the park."

Initially he felt the sort of uneasiness you might get watching a panther in a cage, an incredible force of strength confined in a strange setting.

"Yeah," he replied. "I've seen you, too. You're pretty good."

"Thanks, so are you."

His name was Ernesto, and the only reason he didn't tell Diana that they'd met, even arranged to run together three days later, was because ever since the day she'd tried to accompany him, all talk of runs had been tacitly suppressed, like the presence of an inexorable lover.

This is what happened one night: he'd just brushed his teeth when he saw Diana in the mirror, getting undressed. Always the same display of intimacy, undoing two or three buttons and then tugging her shirt over her head almost scornfully, the way a little girl takes off a frilly dress; always the same annoyance at picking her pants up off the floor after removing them each day, draping them over the back of a chair like a pair of disembodied legs. Diana's life resided in those displays, the repeated rituals, the gestures, but suddenly it was as if she were a stranger to him, and he, in turn, unknown to her. The fact that they'd been married only three months made the whole thing not ironic but sad. How could they do anything but hate each other, he thought, how could two people not end up hating one another, in a home where they had to turn sideways and press into the wall just to pass in the hallway, in a kitchen where more than two was a crowd, in a bed in which to sleep without touching was a miracle. He needed air, space—that was why he ran.

Her orderliness made matters worse. The first time he saw the apartment bare, its walls papered—they later decided to paint them white—it seemed bigger, and more impersonal. In the two months following the wedding, Diana had felt an almost physical need to fill the space. Not a week went by that she didn't make some purchase or change something around.

Bend Pole B into shape indicated in diagram. Slide through the metal grommet, read Diana's translation, cast aside on the table by the diagram of what looked to be a tent. He was beginning to feel that even their exchanges were taking on the clipped, imperative tone of instructions. "You running tomorrow?" "Why?" "We could go to the movies, we haven't been in ages." "I'm running," and then they went to bed, like that, with Diana predictably annoyed and him feeling he'd repeated this routine too often in recent weeks (*Tug firmly on the end of the pole marked F [see diagram] taking care not to wrinkle the floor of the tent*) because Diana, on certain occasions, had become so unlike Diana: a hand reaching through the sheets to his chin, stroking his face, turning it toward her, and then came the foot, the lip, the sheet, the smell of toothpaste, the almost-sweet taste of her neck straining in the characteristic sign of her excitement; "You took your pill, right?" (*Each stake is fed through a rubber loop, which can be pinched open for easier insertion. To ensure that stakes are firmly secured, insert diagonally, angling toward structure*), the unexpected lubricity of an I-love-you, spoken a bit selfishly because she liked to say that in bed, and then her hand following the obligatory path, which he in turn would facilitate by shifting his body and which Diana would accept because she thought he liked it even though she'd never asked, her foot again, her soft inner thigh spreading, on top of him (*If the preceding steps have been followed correctly, the rain cover will fit over the pole frame*) although he didn't like her insistence, and she seemed to forget him for a moment, looking upward, pronouncing his name as if it were another's, and he would think he could fake it, he did once before and she didn't realize, he could do it again, a couple of convulsions, over quickly (*The rain cover is staked to the ground following the same steps. Now you can enjoy your expertly assembled tent, designed to withstand low temperatures and inclement weather*), sheets kicked off that will then have to be back on. Diana's body pulling back, to prolong the pleasure. And now simply wait for the warm tingling to peak and subside, her first (always her first) and then him, accepting the obligatory fleetingness, the joy which, after the ragged breathing, in the end, is not enough.

* * *

Ernesto was on time and dressed as he'd seen him on so many other occasions. For a moment, watching him approach—his slender beauty, his red hair—he was almost jealous. They did some stretching against a bench before starting to run, making small talk about their lives. Ernesto's seemed confined to two years of university, where he studied journalism before dropping out, and many more at his father's greengrocers. His own was embellished with a couple of lies about his degrees and job. He didn't mention Diana because Ernesto hadn't brought up his partner. Whether he even had one, at the time, seemed—like the memory of Diana—utterly superfluous. They were there to run, wasn't that the greater truth? Wasn't this about pleasures that other people couldn't understand?

"Let's not talk about our private lives," he said finally, and Ernesto gave him what he thought was a look of surprise.

"Okay," he said.

Running with Ernesto that first night gave him a strange, pleasant feeling of emptiness, and the silence encircled his pleasure, accentuating it the way a picture frame enhances a painting without adding to it. He felt as though anything but running, anything but the sound of Ernesto's breath beside him, and their synchronized footfalls, had no need to be articulated. The world, in its purest manifestation, was contained there.

Ernesto was only a year younger, which gave them both a sort of fraternal feeling. They both knew, before their first run was over, that they'd meet up again soon, and that after that night, running without the other wouldn't be the same. He could see it in Ernesto's eyes when they said goodbye, exchanging phone numbers.

"I'll call you," Ernesto said.

"Better if I call you; I never know when I'm going to be home. Work and all that, you know how it is."

"Sure."

He felt, after saying this, as if he'd betrayed Diana in some profound and ridiculous way. Why lie? What was he afraid of? He started walking home and then turned to look back one last time. Ernesto was running, fast, down the wide avenue that bordered the park. Then, turning down the second side street, he disappeared like some fictional being.

He called Ernesto for the first time three days later, feeling nervous when he dialed, nervous when a woman answered and asked who was calling; as he told her his name he considered the vast expanse of conversations set in motion when a new voice, a new name, suddenly crops up, asking for a family member.

"One moment," said the woman, and then shouted Ernesto's name.

He was troubled by his own nervousness, and by the fact that he was calling from the office, as though hiding it from Diana. The sounds he heard through the receiver—unknown hallways, unknown doors—made the whole thing more ridiculous, if that was possible.

"How's it going?" Ernesto asked easily, picking up the phone.

"Good."

"I was just thinking about you, actually."

"Oh, yeah?" he asked, feeling the sudden simple elation of one receiving an unexpected gift.

"Yeah. Have you ever run the marathon?"

"Twice," he lied. "You?"

"Just once, last year. I was thinking we could run it together this year. Train together, I mean."

"What's your time?"

"3:04."

"Same as me, more or less. 2:55."

"If we train hard, I think we could run 2:45. But there's only two months till the race."

"So when do we start?"

"Tomorrow, no? This will take a lot of work," Ernesto said.

"Yes," he replied, determination kicking in, gearing up for the plan.

So often, living life gets in the way of expressing it. Particularly after getting in from work, exhaustion weighing him down, he was filled with dread at what had become Diana's habitual question, "What's the matter?" which she now asked as though it were a vaguely affectionate embrace, and which he answered with a predictable, "Nothing," equally listless, equally habitual, as unnecessary as the question that had provoked it. Her reaction looked a lot like eyes adjusting to the dark. Sometimes Diana's love drained him. It was a feeling that started in his stomach, and later he could feel it in his hands, in his gestures. If she tried to touch him there were times he couldn't help but brush her off with distaste; if she asked what the matter was it was worse. There were days he felt like running away. It happened certain evenings, in a certain light, especially since he'd spoken to Ernesto and they'd decided to train for the marathon together: something like the ennui of feeling loved, of having to respond physically to Diana in equal measure, kiss for kiss, touch for touch; it was also the new order of the apartment, which she could navigate blindfolded without bumping into a single piece of furniture: the bedroom, the living room, the bookcases, the collection of porcelain ducks, the bathroom (Diana liked all of the sponges lined up just so), the mirror with a green border she'd made one bored Sunday afternoon. Diana's obsession with order seemed aimed not at the usefulness of knowing where things were, or the simple pleasure of seeing things in their place, but at the establishment of a hierarchy in which she herself was vital.

He thought that perhaps he'd never really known Diana, that maybe she didn't know him either. The fact that they'd dated for eight years before marrying sometimes intensified his unease to the point of exasperation, and he'd

stop to run through all the time they'd been together before
the wedding, searching for antecedents, examining dissatisfactions—no matter how trivial or momentary—that might
justify his current apathy.

"What do you want for dinner?"

"Whatever," and he'd turn on the TV as they sat down,
using the news as an excuse—there had been a terrorist
attack the day before. *The suction filters should be cleaned every four uses*, read the last page of Diana's translation, which
he moved in order to lay the tablecloth, wishing he weren't
there, wishing he were out running with Ernesto, training
for the marathon that now seemed, more than a leisure activity, his great aspiration.

He would never know for certain whether it really was Ernesto. He did know that it looked like him, that for a few
seconds he was absolutely certain that it was him—maybe
it was the T-shirt, or perhaps simply his running style. He
also knew that it altered the course of events in the same way
that something mysterious, almost invisible can sometimes
change a woman's mind, make a man's attempt at seduc-
tion hopeless, and not even she would be able to explain it.
He knew—and some nights he still thought about this—that
that was the reason he didn't call Diana, and he regretted it,
and his regret was utterly futile. He left for the office a little
earlier than usual and caught sight of the back of a runner,
just for a few seconds, going around the bend toward the
park. A redhead, like Ernesto. After the initial shock came

the conviction that it was true: Ernesto was training behind his back. Discovering this was like having his last refuge poisoned.

Over the preceding week, the idea of running the marathon with Ernesto had filled the emptiness Diana produced in him with an agreeable sense of purpose, of purity. And yet the moment he saw Ernesto (though maybe it wasn't him) he felt foolish for having been so naïve the past several days. Ernesto was training behind his back in order to beat him. It was so obvious as to be ridiculous, adolescent almost. Ernesto wasn't telling him that he was training extra, knowing that *he* couldn't possibly run as much since he had a job to go to, and a wife (though Ernesto didn't know that). Even working at the greengrocers was like extra physical training for Ernesto, he thought suddenly, amazed at his own obliviousness, his disadvantage, though more hurt than indignant. He phoned from the office and a woman's voice said that Ernesto wasn't home, to call back later.

"Don't you know where he is?"

"Why? Is it urgent?"

"No."

"I have no idea where he is. When I got in he was gone. Sometimes he leaves early, but he always comes back at lunchtime. Sometimes he goes for a run."

"Thank you."

She'd said it. There it was, the leaden truth. Ernesto had promised not to train without him, had said they'd do everything together from the start so they could see who the better runner really was, and he'd broken his promise. He'd thought, in that instant, that finding out Diana was being unfaithful would have hurt less. Ernesto (though maybe the man he saw wasn't actually Ernesto) had rendered the entire plan meaningless. He didn't tell Diana when he got home because she would never have understood, because no doubt she'd have been upset at the fact that he hadn't mentioned anything about it up until then. Seeing her sitting there at the table by the door, beside the collection of porcelain ducks, finishing a translation, was all the dissuasion he needed, and they had dinner in a silence that was filled, as ever, with her voice, suggesting they go away for a weekend, maybe go to see a movie, or to the theater, or out to dinner.

"I'm suffocating here," she said finally.

Then it was like waking from a dream, except that while in it he'd been perfectly aware of each of his movements. He recalled having stood up from the table when Diana said for the first time that she was suffocating, in a tone clearly tinged with reproach, recalled feeling uneasy at that, and going into the bedroom. He was aware of having looked out the window, as though the nightmare vision of Ernesto might appear yet again, running toward the park, rekindling his obsession over what seemed the worst form of betrayal.

This is what Diana said from the bedroom door:

"What's wrong with us?" And he made no reply. He was aware, after that, of having been hugged openly, with no malice, and of a change in pronoun, which made the question honest, "What's wrong with you? Talk to me,"—and again, at his silence—"I'm suffocating," and also of the fact that suddenly he could not bear the responsibility of Diana, the burden of Diana, this woman breathing on his neck, ruffling his hair, thinking she owned him.

"Why don't we go away this weekend? We can afford it. We could go to the north, or to the beach, the weather's not bad."

He recalled having turned to face her and having grabbed her, hard, by the shoulders, having shouted that he had to train for the marathon, why couldn't she understand that; and Diana had said, "You're hurting me," and that all she did was sit there all day alone in the apartment, never going out, so how could she possibly understand, with the life she led.

"You're hurting me," Diana had repeated, a trace of fear in her voice, as though confronting a strange man for the first time, and he'd realized that he really was hurting her, and felt as if he was waking up when he let go and she took a little step back, half a step, and they stood looking at one another.

"I'm sorry," he said, but he didn't tell her about Ernesto, nor did he say, when they went to bed, that he wanted to cry with anger.

This is how an obsession begins: making almost no noise, like a single off-key note in the middle of a melody. It never does any harm the first time. It hides away, festering like

an unpleasant apparition, reproducing slowly, going unnoticed. Never, until the damage is done, is an obsession
understood. First it spills over into the morning coffee, the
kiss of a woman attempting to repair a relationship, a job
in the probate division of a law firm; it actually seems as
though it's always been there, as though the unpleasantness
of its presence is no different from so many other unpleasant
things, so many other presences. An obsession makes a man
go to the pharmacy for multi-vitamins and take them daily,
thinking the whole world rides on this act, and go running
in the evenings with another man he slowly begins to detest,
almost without even realizing it.

"Come on, grandpa, you're showing your age," says Ernesto, and an obsessed man thinks that *he* is the stronger
of the two, but that it's in his interest for the enemy not to
know this, and to believe his deception has gone unnoticed
(although maybe the man he saw that morning wasn't Ernesto), so an obsessed man smiles and says, "Yeah, yeah,
shut up and run," pretending to be more tired than he in
fact is, knowing he could sprint at any moment and leave
the enemy behind, but preferring to relish his own deceit,
to savor it the way he savors another deceit that no longer
seems real when he comes home, one named Diana, whose
fear has gone unspoken for the past two weeks since he
grabbed her by the shoulders and shouted, feeling no horror
at the sort of behavior that would have horrified another.

The burden of a woman, to a man obsessed, becomes light, almost disappears, because she is not real even though she touches, and smells.

"We could go to a movie tonight," Diana says, "they're showing the kind of movie I love and you hate," and to the woman's great shock the man says yes, and sees a movie, and lets her stroke his arm and kiss him during one of the love scenes, but he does not succumb, doesn't—deep down—consider her real, in the same way that he doesn't consider real anything that separates him not from himself but from that which is now greater than himself and which has no name although it does have repercussions, makes him count calories at breakfast and run secretly in other parks.

He'd always loved running the way a little kid loves gazing up at the sky—irrationally, with no interruption seeming possible. Thinking about that now, with little more than a month until the marathon, he felt a vague sense of sadness, disapproval even. He remembered that when he was fifteen years old he went to every school track meet, and always won. Besting his own record by a second or two back then had the allure of absolute perfection, and the feeling of having beaten himself, through his own effort, was so powerful that the applause was irrelevant. But one day he felt suddenly alone, alone against his time, against his body, against his life, and he stopped running for several months, for as long as the feeling lasted, the self-contained world of running crushing his soul, the loneliness that running condemned him to seeming to have no outside. The feeling was back now, with a twist: Ernesto was his outside, his plan. More than the desire to beat Ernesto's marathon time, what he felt was Ernesto himself rising up before him, against him, the same way Diana (though from a different place) was his outside, rising up against him; both were like a race begun too fast, both like the wall marathoners hit at mile twenty, when they feel suddenly, inexplicably alone and vulnerable, while all the other runners seem to possess a single iron will from which they alone—the weak ones—are excluded, six miles to go and their souls plummet into an exhaustion so complete that they're on the verge of giving up entirely on the very next step, the words "I can't" pounding in their temples with each heartbeat, the same way Diana pounds on the keyboard banging out her translations, (*"Never plug appliance in without ensuring the surface is completely dry"*), "I can't, I can't, I can't" coursing through their arms, so exhausted they hardly swing, the bib number on their backs now seeming absurd, anonymous, almost insulting, Diana repeating her getting-undressed ritual as he brushes his teeth, always draping her pants over the chair the same way, always tugging her shirt off over her head as though vexed, trunk thrashing, Diana—suddenly—no longer seems real (*"ideal for beating eggs, grinding meat, vegetables or making any type of soup or smoothie"*), and Ernesto resides inside of her, despite not being her, not resembling her.

* * *

It happened. And it happened in an absurd way, to boot. She said:

"We have to fix this, fix *us* or . . ."

"What is it about *us* that we have to fix?"

But Diana didn't even turn to him, didn't so much as raise her eyes from the computer, seemed not even to be speaking to him, to be clucking her tongue and grimacing at a typo.

"Or I'm going to leave home, until you make up your mind whether you want to live with me."

"What are you talking about? Of course I want to live with you," he replied with false conviction, which did nothing to quell Diana's solemnity.

"Then show it," she said, and walked into the bedroom.

At that moment it struck him that he was selfish, maybe always had been, in the way he loved Diana. It was true: all too often he treated her as though she herself had no needs, as though her only job, her duty, was to attend to his happiness. This realization did not diminish the aversion he'd felt toward her since the wedding, but it did suddenly save her somehow, lend her some weight. From that day until the following Saturday, Diana became a creature who withdrew into a wounded yet expectant silence. Every time he got home and found her at the computer, every time they had dinner or breakfast, there came a moment when she couldn't help but give him a languid look, a sort of *love me* entreaty made more uncomfortable by the silence, a look in which it seemed to him that the old Diana was hiding, as though suddenly embarrassed to reveal herself in his presence. She was like a long-distance runner who's trying to feign exhaustion, he thought, but is betrayed by a quick move and, on being discovered, becomes vulnerable.

And yet Diana's weakness, despite how much it irked him now, had been one of the things he'd always found attractive about her. Or perhaps more than her actual weakness it was the way she displayed it, was unembarrassed by it. It had always given him a sense of superiority, like someone who, deep down, can see condescending affection as the only way to respond to a creature unable to survive without his help. It was the same sort of superiority that he now felt over Ernesto, whose simple mind was—with the exception of his love of running—as easily satisfied as that of a child.

Ernesto was nothing but a pretty boy used to hitting it off with women, a dullard, a thin wiry kid whose optimism was so unassailable that at times it was impossible not to question his intelligence. The world, in Ernesto's eyes, was simple and carefree: he ate if he was hungry, slept if he was tired, ran if he felt like running. It was like he'd never regretted anything. And yet his empty-headed happiness was no less happy than any other. There was no cliché Ernesto did not somehow embody; his judgments on serious topics were always others' judgments, dim-witted but well-intentioned truisms—and yet this seemed enough for him.

"I'm not too bright but I'm no moron," he said, and that

seemed the best definition of Ernesto, especially when he said it himself while they were running.

Hearing this, and realizing that Ernesto was embarrassed to discuss certain things because he felt outsmarted, had given him a sense of superiority from the start. Seeing Ernesto on a covert run that morning (though it might not have been him), realizing, then that Ernesto might in fact be in better shape than he was, made him constantly search for ways to affirm his superiority over the wiry redhead who sometimes left him lagging slightly behind, who made him think (though not like this, not clearly) he wasn't actually going to win without putting in some extra training, without running at night, too.

Twenty-nine days until the marathon. That was what Ernesto had said before they started their run that evening, and he felt like he'd been beaten already. Not by Ernesto, or Diana, but by himself, by his everyday life, the image of himself in his everyday life was beating him in his real one, rendering it absurd. He ran furiously, desperately, that evening.

"Why are you starting out so fast? You want some kind of prize?" Ernesto asked, his voice tinged with irritation, indignation almost. "We can't keep up this pace for more than ten kilometers. Are you nuts?"

"No."

"It's not a fifteen-hundred, it's a marathon. Remember?"

He made no reply, feeling the silent satisfaction of passing the other runners in the park. Continuing to pick up the pace gave him an intensely powerful feeling, especially since Ernesto was behind, only by a foot or two, but it was a foot or two that he strived to maintain each time Ernesto tried to adapt to his pace.

"You're handling the pace just fine!" he shouted, trying to keep his breath. "Haven't been training without telling me, have you?"

"What?"

"You heard me!"

"No, I haven't, but I wouldn't be ashamed of it if I had."

They were flying, and almost shouting, which made other runners turn in surprise to stare.

"Don't lie; I saw you the other day, a couple weeks ago!"

"Who, me?"

Ernesto tried to catch up, to look him in the face, but he picked up the pace even more.

"Yeah, you!"

It was like a hundred-meter sprint.

"Are you crazy?" Ernesto shouted. "I'm out of here, man."

"I'll see you at the marathon!"

"What?"

"See you at the marathon!" he shouted, enraged, sensing Ernesto stop. He himself did not stop. In fact, he sped up slightly. He was alone again. Alone against his own time, against his own body. *What if I didn't stop? What if I never stopped running?* he thought. Each stride, each sensation closer to fatigue, to exhaustion, seemed to pull him deeper into some nameless virgin territory, one that nobody but him could possibly understand, and yet it was also somehow frightening. He thought life would make sense if he could feel this way permanently, without resting or getting tired, thought *If only I could never stop running*, like it was the greatest wish, the greatest possible joy, and now that Ernesto was no longer there, the joy seemed even more pure. His knee began to hurt but he didn't stop running. He had to plumb the depths of this satisfaction, to gulp it down if necessary, to die inside it. Exhaustion began to cloud his eyes but he tried to run faster still. And then he tripped. The fall was clean and white and left his hands bloody and encrusted with sand. His knee was bleeding too. When he got home Diana let out a frightened little cry.

"I fell," he said, determined to offer no further explanation.

"Are you alright?"

"Fine."

He went into the bathroom and locked the door. Standing in the shower, under a stream of cold water, without knowing why, he began to laugh.

He didn't see Ernesto again. He ran for four hours on Sunday with almost no rest—and then again on Monday, and Tuesday. Wednesday he realized he performed better late at night, so began running then too. Diana spoke only of trivial things—what they should have to eat, English words that meant different things in different contexts. She no longer asked where he was going, no longer suggested movies or weekends in a hotel in the north. It was as if, after having first tried locking herself in a prison of expectant silence, she'd thrown in the towel and now looked on her failure with no sorrow. She seemed not to weigh anything when she got into bed at night, not to move through the apartment, an apartment that now more than ever was but a extension of herself: wedding photos, the porcelain duck collection, the green-framed bathroom mirror, the encyclopedia on the bookshelf, all as unmoving as Diana at her computer. "How's it going?" "Almost done," but never really done because when she finished she'd go back to the beginning and edit, comparing her translation with the original. "Come on. Who cares about an 'in' instead of an 'on' when you're talking about a kitchen appliance?" "I do." And this response (more the tone than the words themselves) was the incontrovertible proof that Diana was also struggling, often unsuccessfully, to exclude him from a realm in which she was now perhaps starting to feel him unnecessary. The pang he felt for the Diana of old, however, the one who needed him, was not strong enough to keep him from training. The idea of the marathon now structured everything so rigidly that thinking of anything else seemed preposterous. Whether or not he sometimes felt guilty for neglecting Diana was a matter that lost absolutely all texture when he was getting ready for a run.

Those days were like a return to adolescence, when air was nothing but a time to beat, his body a machine from which to extract optimal performance. He realized that he didn't even think on runs, or if he did it was in code, a code he couldn't have explained: the irrationality of a perfectly conditioned machine. He thought of his body the way a racecar driver thinks of his car, as an object that both belongs to him and doesn't, an object that could be dismantled piece by piece, one that, when assembled, he didn't understand beyond knowing that it was not entirely his own.

It was Wednesday when his knees began to hurt, and there were only twenty days until the marathon. He knew he should rest, knew that rest was often beneficial to performance, knew that knee pain, if ignored, could lead to serious injury; he knew all of those things and yet that night he ran even longer than usual—six hours. The following day when his alarm went off he was utterly spent. Couldn't move. He told Diana, expecting her to lecture him, but she didn't.

"Do you want me to call the doctor?"

"I have no strength, it's like I have absolutely no strength," he said, as though shocked by his own words, but Diana didn't respond to his shock and he got out of bed and gave her a desperate look. "I can't run like this. The marathon is less than three weeks away."

"Oh, the marathon."

"You must be glad. You must just be relishing this."

"Of course not. Is that really what you think?" He didn't answer, because doing so would have meant acknowledging his guilt. And she said, "Well. Should I call the doctor or not?" in a different tone, a warmer tone, as though deep down she couldn't help but pity him.

"Yes."

The desperation he felt all morning waiting for the doctor to arrive, and then in the hours following his visit, was too profound to articulate. The doctor asked him about his runs, listened to his heart, and concluded that his state of weakness was simply due to the overtraining he'd put himself through.

"Five days' complete rest," he declared. "Even muscle mass has its limit; if you subject it to too much intense stress, or to constant stress, it gets weaker rather than stronger. Not even professional athletes spend that many hours training."

He despised the doctor for his admonishing tone, his apostle-of-common-sense demeanor, despised Diana for blindly agreeing. He turned away as they spoke, so as not to have to see them.

Spending those days at home was like discovering a new city within the one he thought he knew. The city, in this case, was Diana, and although he'd pictured her routines, actually seeing them all performed was completely new. The first day was the worst: he spent it waiting, all afternoon, for Diana to reprimand him, which she did not. This at first seemed a reprieve, but as the hours crept by, the fact that she didn't reproach him for anything began to warp his outlook even more than not being able to train for the marathon. What was going on? Didn't she care, or what? He, on the other hand, discovered the world his wife inhabited, a world of footsteps to the kitchen to get a soda before sitting down with her translation, of classical music, Tchaikovsky drifting in from the hallway.

"Beethoven and Mozart are too distracting," she said, and at times the sound of the piano was strangely beautiful, strangely melancholic, in a way that seemed gentle even at its most exalted, in the same way that not having known Diana did these things when she was alone seemed strangely sad or melancholic—not to have known she preferred Tchaikovsky, for example, or that she took a break to watch the news and smoke a cigarette, sitting down with the sort of pre-planned methodical pleasure a person like Diana surrendered to as if it were a haven she'd been looking forward to all morning. Being at home was, in a way, like being a spy, having access to a level of intimacy he didn't feel entitled to, as though given that he'd excluded Diana from the intimacy of his running she were perfectly in her rights to now exclude him from her own, from her cigarette break while watching the news and Tchaikovsky accompanying the dull thunk of her enormous dictionary being closed on the table.

Discovering his weakness left him wallowing in a world of melancholy. Hearing Diana's music, hearing her fingers on the keyboard, brought him back to their dating years, when happiness was simple and acceptable, satisfactory despite following pre-established patterns imposed by others. He'd never been melancholic. Had always seen that territory of the soul as a burden surrendered to by the weak out of sheer indolence and found the pleasure others took in their own pain sick—especially the tender, mawkish sort of pain wrought by melancholia. So discovering that he, too, had these feelings was something he immediately chose to attribute—as the doctor had said—to overtraining, although it carried on for several more days, growing stronger with each passing hour, because there was something in Diana's silence that resembled the desire to give him another chance, a sort of renewed expectancy that dared not be spoken.

A photograph. He discovered it by chance, dismantling the picture frame on his nightstand out of boredom. Diana was working in the living room, as always, and his third day of immobility was starting to seem unbearable. The frame opened with a little click, revealing another, older photo hidden behind the one on display. He slid it out indifferently. He remembered the picture, it was one he'd kept on a bookshelf in his bedroom during their last year of courtship. A large patio, in Paris, beside a plant. His arm over Diana's shoulders, pulling her in tightly. He was kissing her, and she was smiling. He felt strangely moved holding it up, bringing it closer to his eyes for a better look. It was from a trip they'd taken to visit one of Diana's friends, a year before the wedding. Even if they seemed completely different now, the pulsating, almost violent truth of the snapshot, the discovery (not the memory but the discovery) that he'd been that man and Diana that woman, seemed to have no background. He called her. Shouted her name, Diana, as though it had changed. And she, from the living room, asked what he wanted.

"Come here," he replied. "Look at this."

She sat on the bed beside him and smiled on seeing the photograph.

"Where was it?"

"Right here, in the frame, behind the picture of you." A look something like compassion flickered in Diana's eyes and then disappeared suddenly, as though it had never been, as though she hadn't even been aware of it when she turned to look at him.

"What are you thinking?" she asked, but he didn't answer, because answering would have been giving in to sadness, to the disappointment that had crossed Diana's eyes, like a train passing a station where it's best not to get off. He put one hand on her hip and with the other touched her breast. Her saliva tasted of Coke when she kissed him as she lay back on the bed.

An obsession can have a woman's shape and touch, contours into which a smell recedes, disappears for a moment, only to waft up again later, with a movement. Admitting its existence, saying it out loud, is not the first step toward recovery and serves only to make it visible. An obsessed man accepts his obsession before the naked body of his wife when he wishes she were not there, when he suddenly finds absurd the disarray wrought by excited lovemaking—the clothes strewn across the bed and floor—sets his gaze on one of her shoes, which has landed upside down by the door, and finds it absurd in the same way that his pajamas are absurd, balled into a shapeless mass beneath the sheets. There's no use voicing this dissatisfaction; it's there, in the breathing of a woman named Diana who turns to embrace him before putting her clothes back on, in the way she looks at him while fastening her bra, in the silence of a woman who suddenly feels cheated, or perhaps feels the shame of realizing she's just done something ridiculous.

An obsessed man cannot, in these circumstances, do anything but once again open the frame that was on his nightstand and hide the photograph that would have been best left undiscovered. He wishes he weren't there, just as he wishes he weren't causing the woman pain. On the other side of the window there must be another man, down there training. If only he could put into words what he feels it would be almost like thinking clearly, but he cannot think clearly. The man he has to beat in the marathon is an extension of himself, a prolongation of his previous life rising up against the absurdity of his current life. If he could admit this perhaps it would all be easier. He cannot. The woman leaves without a sound and the man hears her turn off the music that, he only noticed then, had been playing. It occurs

to the man that, like the music, the woman too is more no-
ticeable by her absence. He feels anxiety constrict his throat,
is anxious to run, to hear the rhythm of his feet pounding
the ground in the park. He imagines the beginning of the
marathon, the starting gun like a sound that instantly cur-
dles his blood, electrifies it. The woman no longer exists.
The world does not exist.

He ran the following day and, though weaker than normal,
could tell his body was regaining some of the strength from
his early training. This made him feel better for a moment,
and forget Diana's silent recrimination for a few hours. The
remaining two weeks before the marathon passed swiftly,
in the way that identical days do. He worked until five,
changed right at the office, and ran from there to the park;
four hours later he returned home, ate copiously and went
to bed. He doesn't remember the Diana of those days; if he
does it's only with the haziness of something both necessary
and invisible. It was as though, at the same time his muscles
were regaining strength, something in her were permanently receding, and she were being ruled out, disappearing to
the point that he now no longer remembered her although
he knew she was there when he got home, that she got into
bed at the same time he did, breathed the same air he did
when going to sleep. He recalls Diana getting into bed the
night before the marathon, recalls her perfectly ambiguous

expression when he said that the following day was the big day, and the way she then got out of bed sadly on that Saturday.

He remembers her saying "good luck" from the bathroom when she heard him open the door to leave, remembers thinking she was lying, that perhaps Diana could only lie those words, even if she truly wanted to say them.

He had no trouble finding Ernesto among the small crowd forming with the hopes of obtaining a privileged spot at the start. They saw one another in line for bib numbers and waited for each other so they could start together, not a single word to misconstrue their silence. He felt strong, and excited, and his sense of strength and excitement only increased over the more than thirty minutes between the time the professional athletes took off and when they themselves were allowed to start. The pack of runners breathed like a single furious animal dangling from strings, and although this would seem a source of unity, they couldn't even touch without becoming vexed; the brush of an elbow, a leg, was like the prick of a needle on hypersensitive skin. Ernesto murmured something he didn't catch and they looked straight at one another for the first time. They sweated not from exertion but the expectation of exertion, a tense misshapen group in which no one spoke but everyone had the same look in their eyes, the same way of constantly wiping their hands dry, of breathing. The starting gun had signaled the beginning of something unreal, the screams of spectators at the barricades seemed to come from inside a cave, someplace far-off and incongruous. The mass of runners opened and closed and then opened again, like viscera ingesting. From time to time the barricades narrowed the course slightly and their fear of coming up on a slower runner made them run elbows out, for protection, occasionally knocking into one another for no real reason.

What happened then resides in the realm of total ambiguity. He'll never know if he saved himself or someone else did. The first man to trip was just a few feet ahead, and he himself was looking the other way at the time. All he knows is that he didn't trip over him, that something (maybe himself, maybe his own intuition) made him leap. Afterward—hearing the inevitable sound of runners colliding behind him, the shock of the crowd at this unforeseen spectacle—he thought that it might have been Ernesto who grabbed his arm, averting him from a fall. Perhaps the act of believing himself saved by Ernesto is what suddenly, and more vehemently than ever, turned Ernesto into the enemy; or perhaps it was thinking that he'd saved himself and Ernesto had done nothing to help. It didn't really matter.

The first ten miles were like his eight years of dating Diana; every move, every reaction seemed predicated on what was expected of them, and that predictability both negated and transcended them as individuals, placing them in a higher order. He thought that any one of the runners breathing there beside him could, at the time, have shouted with joy, and yet the truth was they felt no joy; but the mo-

mentous sound of their footfalls, the torrent of feet pounding the ground, made them a force of nature, a stampede
of wild horses that had suddenly taken the city. Allowing
himself to be flooded by that sensation was like surrendering
his freedom to a more powerful force and enjoying the sub-
mission, for it offered him the happiness of being unable to
make a mistake, no matter what he did. A mile or two later
the real marathon would begin, the one where they'd each
be on their own, where their solitude would open and close
like a vast expanse of nothing, or of nonsense.

It was at mile eleven that he felt younger and stronger
than he in fact was, and attempted a breakaway that Ernesto seemed to concede, lagging slightly behind. For over
three miles his solitude wrought havoc, like an avalanche of
absurdity raining down: he was ahead, true, but it was as
if his goal were behind him, as if beating Ernesto without
being able to see him defeated the whole point, and this
threw him off, made him lose his stride. If he came up on a
steep incline, he sped up too much out of anxiousness and
was exhausted afterward. He lost his breath for several seconds and then caught it, but didn't stop panting until he felt
Ernesto beside him once more. Ernesto's bib number was
1476 and he stared at it as though doing so somehow made
Ernesto less real and gave *him* more strength than he actually had. He did the same with Diana, but now the whole
world came down to keeping Ernesto from getting more
than a foot and a half ahead, everything was concentrated
there, everything—the spectators breathing on either side

of the guardrails, Diana's translations, her body sinking into bed almost weightlessly beside him, her palm upturned on the sheet, asking in an absurd almost adolescent way (unbelievable, really) for something she didn't dare ask for any other way—for him to turn to her, to make love to her; but how could he make love to her the night before the marathon, how (and Diana should have known this already) was he supposed to do that the night before a race, knowing how much of his energy it would sap? He'd turned onto his side to avoid looking at her and repeated, "Tomorrow's the big day," and she had said, "Yes," trying not to make any noise as she pulled her hand away, as though ashamed even to have asked. He pitied her silence then, and decided to go ahead, to make love to Diana quickly, and then turn away as soon as possible and go to sleep. But he wasn't going to say so openly, after the overture she'd made, which is why he reached out a foot, to touch hers beneath the sheets. Mile fifteen and there was the image of Diana, again and again, and Ernesto, in the silence that once more turned into his foot searching for hers and not finding it, because she too had pulled away so as not to look at him, just as Ernesto was now pulling away so as not to look at him; Ernesto's legs before him now exactly like Diana's legs the night before, hip sinking into the sheet like a soft wave of flesh, him on the verge of saying her name, on the verge of saying "Diana" but not managing to do it, just as now he did not manage to catch up to Ernesto, to run beside him.

Knowing about the wall in advance made it no easier to

endure when he hit it at mile twenty. It started with a sense of regret over his breakaway and then made its way to his arms, his shoulders, his head. If only he hadn't thought so much about Diana over the past few miles, if he'd focused more on the race, he might feel less exhausted now. Ernesto's energy, by contrast, seemed boundless. He'd maintained the same pace, the same breathing pattern, since catching up over four miles ago; suddenly the man's resistance seemed inhuman. Someone poured a bottle of water over his head, soaking his shirt and bib. 1476, he read, one-thousand four-hundred seventy-six, as Ernesto pulled decisively ahead—a foot and a half, three feet, five, the words *I can't* pounding in his temples, along with 1476, and Diana scoffing at him, because she'd undoubtedly have scoffed at him, at his failure, in these circumstances. He thought about quitting, giving up when Ernesto couldn't see him, and would have done so behind mile marker 21 had Ernesto not turned back to look at him. He felt Ernesto's eyes lash across him like a whip, and then the distance between them shrank, which made no sense.

"Only five more miles," he said, as though speaking these words aloud might somehow help him, might magically reduce the stamina required to keep up the pace. When Ernesto was once again beside him, he got the feeling he'd forced something, that there was something completely unnatural about the way Ernest had (possibly) held back, as if it had been a voluntary act, as if Ernesto had waited for him. He wanted to say so but did not. He kept running—he thought—because he had to finish the race, not because he had to beat Ernesto. He'd realized three miles earlier that it was going to be impossible to make his goal and this realization, along with everything else, including the memory of Diana, seemed totally ludicrous. The feeling lasted a few miles, but as he passed the 24-mile marker something inside him snapped and every ounce of his determination was once again thrown into the singular aim of beating Ernesto. He attempted to pull away yet again but couldn't manage to get more than a few feet ahead. If anyone had asked, he'd have said that he hated him. Hated Ernesto, and himself, and the crowds shouting from behind the barricades, and his satisfaction at the idea of beating him, and the idea of being beaten; and the hate strangled him, like a fury. He wanted to destroy Ernesto and destroy himself; to beat him and then die when the race was over.

He ran the last two miles in a state of near hysteria, jaw clenched so tight it hurt. In the last five hundred meters Ernesto gave a little sprint, as though attempting to prove something (but prove what?) and then returned to his side. Again he heard the crowd screaming, and again he hated them for pouring water over him. The finish line appeared in the distance, ugly and absurd, and brilliant. Attempting to pull ahead of Ernesto he lost his balance and almost fell, and it was only because he leaned into Ernesto, pushing him, that he did not. He crossed the finish line with the utter dissatisfaction of a man with no idea why he's done what he's done, and turning to look back all he could see was a group of people gathered where Ernesto lay sprawled, fifty feet away. "I won," he thought.

"I beat him," he said, as though pronouncing the words might purge the dissatisfaction suddenly rising in his throat. He thought, guiltily, that he didn't care about Ernesto falling. And yet he wanted to see him, not to gloat over having beaten him but to see if the satisfaction he'd sought (and not found) might come when he saw Ernesto on the ground. They wouldn't let him through, and he felt so weak that all it took to dissuade his attempts was a gentle push.

Going home was like starting an incredibly long, boring game all over again, and when Diana opened the door he told her the truth:

"I won."

"I know," she replied.

He pushed past her at the door and walked toward the hall without caring about her words, which hung mysteriously in the air, there by the front door, like a riddle that cannot or must not be solved. He walked into the bedroom and flopped down on the bed. A few seconds later Diana appeared in the doorway. She said his name once. Twice. Three times.

The same pointlessness he'd felt winning the race rose in his throat again on hearing Diana's voice, calling his name. He hoped she would not come to him, would leave him in peace, and at the same time life splintered into ridiculous plans (to go running again), fears (maybe it wasn't Ernesto he'd seen that one morning), dissatisfactions (Diana's kind-

ness colliding with his single-mindedness like a gentle wave).
She said his name once more, then came over to the bed,
sat down beside him. Suddenly he couldn't bear her hand
in his hair, couldn't bear the gentle way she said his name
yet again, and, after withstanding a few seconds turned to
her brusquely.

"Would you please just leave me alone!" he shouted,
and Diana's face froze in a pathetic expression, a blend of
disbelief, fear, and the urge to cry.

She walked out without making a sound, as though she
had no body, not turning to look at him. He let himself sink
into a heavy black suffocating sleep.

A month later they divorced, the way so many couples do in
their first years of marriage—with a sense of assumed failure, and embarrassment. Diana's absence was this:

Silence in the bathroom before getting into bed.

Empty space in the closets.

The memory of voices and photographs.

She left one Wednesday afternoon when the apartment
was sweltering in the springtime heat, and before walking
out, absurdly, lowered the blinds to keep the sun out, the
same way a suicide victim folds clothes never to be worn
again before jumping off a cliff. Her sister dealt with the
legal procedures and, after an initial period of silence during
which she made no attempt to disguise her hatred, was also
the one to accompany the lawyer, to come over with the
documents—pre-signed by Diana, who was no doubt out

of town, far away, safe from him—to be signed. He learned through the sister, whose malicious intent was to see him suffer rather than to provide objective information, that Diana was seeing a psychologist, and on meds; yet rather than pity, he felt a sort of guilt-ridden happiness that she was being kept away from him, preparing to start a new life in which perhaps she could be happy herself.

Running was the great liberation, especially in those days when the silence at home, which he'd begun to grow used to, made going outside seem like the only possible act. If anyone had asked if he was happy he wouldn't have known how to respond. Perhaps by saying that he felt empty, and that emptiness was, if not happiness, then the closest thing to a state of calm he'd ever known, a calm that didn't need to be spoken or shared, and keeping it to himself made it no less happy but did (strangely) make it more real. He realized that all of the states in which he'd previously believed himself happy had led him to share his joy, to speak it, and that this new state seemed more real because he no longer felt that need, because voicing it, sharing it, would have added nothing to the simple satisfaction of running.

Slowly, something inside him retracted, his need for others shrank, became miniscule, froze, and while the presence of other people never actively bothered him, he did try to get away from them as soon as possible, and thought they were as unnecessary as he himself felt, and accepted that he was.

In the first four months of Diana's absence he sank into

an abyss in which he felt he'd never ultimately know himself. The people around him commented on how much he'd changed, attributing it to the divorce, when the truth was that Diana hadn't caused the change and had in fact been the sole obstacle keeping from embracing this new state, which he seemed naturally suited to. And when he did, it was not out of remorse but because her absence was still too real, too palpable, and now he saw that it was precisely Diana's absence which made him good, purified him, transforming him into something better than he had been.

It was early summer when, stretching before a run, he bumped into Ernesto in the park. They hadn't seen one another since the marathon, and after spotting him in the distance, they looked at one another, and he felt neither pleasure nor anger but something akin to the sensation that made his palms sweat when he came across a photo of Diana—a feeling that, though not unpleasant, brought back the almost-embarrassed memory of who he'd been. He didn't approach Ernesto because he wouldn't have known what to say, but nor did he look away. Instead he kept stretching, and in a few minutes saw Ernesto coming over. It was as though no time had passed, as though Ernesto were going to say, like he had the day they first met, "You run, don't you? I've seen you here in the park, lots of times," but instead stopped before him, silent, and stood threateningly, until he himself finally spoke.

"What do you want?"

"I want to tell you the truth."

Then a new silence, justified in part by the solemn tone Ernesto had used on speaking those words. A runner passed by, quickly, and they both stared after him until the man turned at some bushes. It was hot out.

"You know full well you didn't beat me at the marathon, you know I let you win," Ernesto continued, wearing an expression of utter revulsion, or wounded pride, and then waited in silence as though daring him to deny it. Which he did not, because suddenly, it seemed equally meaningless either way, whether he'd won or lost. Conceding to Ernesto now added nothing, just as the sunlight in the park, or the afternoon heat, added nothing.

"I bet you want to know why."

"Sure," he replied despite feeling no curiosity, because he knew that Ernesto wanted to tell him.

"Diana asked me to. Diana was the one who wanted me to let you win." Ernesto had spoken quickly, awaiting his reaction, and seemed to delight in it, smiling as the obvious shock set in.

"Diana?"

"Yeah. She knew we ran together. She used to come watch sometimes, but you never even noticed."

"Diana," he said, thinking he'd have been less shocked had Diana herself appeared then and there and confessed.

"She thought if you won it would fix things between the two of you."

"She told you that?"

"Yes. She was desperate. Cried when she came to see me."

Some part of Ernesto was taking pleasure in relaying these details, as if finally this were his victory and he wanted to relish it, savor it. He felt disgusted by Ernesto, more for knowing so much about Diana's life than for accusing him of having caused her unhappiness.

"Anything else you'd like to tell me, Ernesto?"

"Yeah. You make me sick."

They heard the breathing and quick steps of a runner but neither turned to look. They felt the heat again now, as though the air were reacting to the density of their expressions. Ernesto left without another word, and he waited in vain for him to turn, for a chance to get one last look at him.

Night was falling on the seventh of May in the best of possible worlds. Running was the only, and the purest, and the most absurd of options.

DESCENT

ALL AT ONCE she became aware of how silent the afternoon was, as though silence, all at once, had been dropped into the middle of the living room, onto the picture of Mamá with corkscrew curls at the almost impossible age of twenty, there among her and Manuel's and the children's things. Mamá had left her the picture in a prideful fit, a month ago, in part because she liked the photo but mostly because she was irritated that there was no image of her on display in the living room and there was one of Manuel's mother. So there she was now: elegant, absurd, out of place, not matching any of the furniture, fighting to be seen—so Mamá.

The words she'd just heard on the phone, the frightened voice of the caregiver (unmistakably South American, possibly overreacting) had left her with that sense of silence, and she felt a bit guilty for not grabbing her purse and running straight for the hospital, as she had other times in similar situations. The Señora, the caregiver had said, well, she slipped in the shower, and since she was so, well, ah, so particular, so private about these things, even though she made a loud bang and began wailing immediately, in order to get to her they had to wait for the ambulance to arrive and break the lock on the bathroom door. Now the Señora was in the hospital. If she waited a bit longer still before leaving home, it was because something seemed to hold her there. Mamá herself, perhaps, in black and white, staring out from the shelf at age twenty, smiling a head-tilted studio smile, a lean-this-way smile, although in her mother's case it must have been the other way around: Mamá telling the photographer exactly what she wanted or didn't want, because this was the picture she'd given Papá when they'd been dating for one year (Papá, always the memory of his funeral that almost didn't seem like a memory); that was in the postwar years and there was no money for frivolities.

But that afternoon something had happened. And it wasn't that she was afraid Mamá would make them all go see her—her and Manuel and the kids, Antonio and Luisa, even María Fernanda from all the way in Valencia—for nothing, for a chance to show them the enormous bruise and demand the affection to which she felt entitled, but that suddenly she got the feeling something had happened to Mamá, it was something about having her mother's thousand faces (which were perhaps all one) there again, one minute authoritarian and the next not, like a collection of fans in a display case.

She gave Mamá's name at hospital reception and felt guilty on being informed that her mother had received emergency care. There were people waiting for the elevator so she ran up the stairs.

"How are you?" she asked, opening the door, and saw her mother in bed, a doctor beside her seemingly waiting for someone to hand him a thermometer.

"Daughter," she said pitifully, and then pointed to the doctor so he could supply a more scientific response.

"You mother's fractured her hip in two places. It's a clean break but it will be very difficult to fuse."

"Because of my degenerative arthritis, isn't that right, doctor?"

"Because of your age, yes."

That tiny snippet of conversation was so Mamá, or at least such a big part of her. She was wearing an ugly sky-blue gown over her brace. The semidarkness of the room accentuated the almost purple bags under her eyes, filled tiny veins that made them look like some weird kind of moss growing beneath her skin. She lay there, arms splayed, palms up, and this, combined with her pallor, made her look crucified.

"Have you called María Fernanda?"

"No, not yet. Does it hurt?"

"Like dogs eating me alive."

"Now, now."

"And Antonio, call Antonio too."

The doctor left without making any noise, a white ghost, assuring them he'd check back in later. Mamá's robe—

which had probably been used to cover her up while they were getting her out of the tub—was in a plastic bag on an armchair.

"Daughter, I have one disaster after another," Mamá said, beginning to whimper.

"Well, if you would let the girl help you bathe . . ."

"That girl has no shame, she's a thief. You need to fire her and find me another."

"You say this every time, and no one's ever stolen a thing from you; if you're talking about your brooch, it'll turn up next week in the place you least expect."

"Her room is a pigsty."

"What do you care what her room is like as long as the rest of the house is clean?"

"And she spends all day on the phone to Venezuela."

"Well don't let her . . ."

She tried to prolong the conversation, not out of any desire to discuss the caretaker, but to keep Mamá from turning to her ailments. Meanwhile she took the robe out of the bag, the maroon robe with her mother's initials, M. A. A., embroidered in gold: María Antonia Alonso, *doña* María Antonia Alonso as the workers called her back when Alonso Woodworks still existed, as As Joaquín had called her, as Antonio himself had been forced to call her when he started working at the factory after deciding to quit school.

Now the robe seemed more Mamá than Mamá herself, or at least more like the old Mamá, less pitiful. It wasn't simply old age that revolted her but Mamá's old age in particular, and perhaps the fear that her own would be much the same. Guiltily, it struck her that she'd rather die than end up like this, like Mamá was now. When she left the hospital to go and pick up a few essentials (toothbrush, pills, a decent towel) she inhaled the cold outside air with relief. She took a taxi and, on the way to Mamá's, thought about Manuel's mother's death, six years earlier. The hospital had made her think of it—every time she walked into a hospital she thought about it, about how, that last week in Bilbao, she hadn't wanted to leave his mother's bedside, hadn't wanted to stop holding her hand, had kissed her over and over. The smell had been the same, and the impersonal feel of the room, and yet she'd done those things effortlessly, as though utterly devoted to performing a perfectly natural act, a just act.

This afternoon, on the other hand, before leaving the hospital room, when Mamá had asked for a kiss, she'd given it almost numbly, almost forcing herself, that was how she'd kissed Mamá, and that wasn't right because a fractured hip at her age could really be quite serious. She decided to make the calls from Mamá's, that would be best, and everyone would be home because it was Saturday, and it was afternoon; Antonio would be too tired from working all week to go out and María Fernanda, according to Mamá, had the flu.

With Antonio it was easier not to pretend. He was still stinging from his blowup with Mamá over Christmas and all he asked was how she was and in what room.

"Are you going to go see her?"

"Yeah, tomorrow."

"She's in bad shape," she said, and would have liked to think she'd said it consciously, but this wasn't true. Her words, intended simply to avoid a goodbye she imagined would be more awkward than usual, had opened a realm of possibilities she was afraid to assess. Of course she was in bad shape, anyone her age who broke a hip was in bad shape, but that wasn't what her words had meant; they'd been more like a silent pact between the two of them—the victims—and the subtle unspoken way they realized this incriminated them.

"Then I'll definitely go tomorrow," Antonio said, and they hung up.

María Fernanda didn't pick up until at least the seventh ring, flu-wrought exhaustion obvious in her voice.

"Mamá broke her hip," she blurted, and then before her sister had time to ask: "She fell in the shower."

"Did she get help quickly?"

"It took some time because she'd locked the bathroom door so they had to break the lock first."

"Honestly. I don't know what we're paying that girl for. She's supposed to be there to help Mamá," María Fernanda said, indignant, her weak tone having vanished.

"Mamá is the one who doesn't let herself be helped," she replied, aware that she was defending the caretaker almost without knowing what had happened.

"Mamá is no longer of an age or in a position to say

what she wants or doesn't want; she's got to be told what to do and that's that."

"Are you trying to blame me for this? Is that what you want?"

"What I want is for you to be on top of things."

"Easy for you to say. You're the one in Valencia."

"Look, let's not start." María Fernanda fell silent for a second, as though in fact what she really would have liked was to start, to have the same old argument, and the two of them realized that even at a time like this, they couldn't help but forget about Mamá and fight.

This conversation, too, had something odd about it. Usually she called María Fernanda from home, sitting in the living room with the door closed, but doing it now, from Mamá's, tinged their words with the flavor of childhood arguments, of hissy fits and adolescent desperation. Before her, in a large silver frame, was the enlargement of a photo she'd have liked to destroy: the two of them in bathing suits—María Fernanda's a bikini, hers a one-piece—laughing, aged twenty, on a beach in Cádiz. To be more precise, María Fernanda was laughing and she was looking at her, smiling in imitation, wearing her photo-face, the face Manuel said she wore every time anyone aimed a camera in her direction. The picture brought back the feeling of dependence on María Fernanda she'd had all those years, with an intensity she thought forgotten. Despite the fact that *she* was the older of the two, a year and a half older in fact, María

Fernanda was the extrovert, the one who made phone calls, who always ended up explaining things to her. Out of her sister's reach she'd always felt better, but when she was with her—until she met Manuel and then married him two years later—she invariably took on an idiotic quality, the dimwitted bashfulness on display in the photo.

As though playing a game, as though acting out the roles in a tragedy, she'd spent those years playing the responsible sister. She expressed shock at María Fernanda's sexual relations with a boy from Somontes not because she was in fact shocked (she herself had almost slept with Manuel) but because acting her part obliged her to be shocked, to believe blindly, even, that her shock was authentic. She'd always found contemplating other people's sexuality distasteful and María Fernanda's was no exception. If anyone were to blame for this it was Mamá, she thought. Too pretty to be a widow and too intrepid to run a factory during those years when she'd always remember her mother as what she was—not Mamá but doña María Antonia Alonso. Joaquín, if he'd ever in fact truly been necessary, was nothing but a pushover, a puppet required for respectability and perhaps Mamá's greatest creation. What could be better, after Papá's death—though this belief implied a malicious intent that may have been absent—than taking the first country boy she could find and making him general manager of the factory? Wasn't that a way of making clear, to those who knew how to read it, that she had in fact been the one behind the scenes taking care of everything the whole time? Wasn't it a way of saying that even Papá was replaceable? The deferential tone she used with Joaquín in the early years had something imperious about it, something disparaging—like those Roman emperors' wives who felt no shame disrobing in front of slaves because they didn't even see them as human—just as María Fernanda's silence on the phone now had something imperious and disparaging about it, as though intellectual superiority had led her to abort a discussion that wasn't getting anywhere.

"You are spending the night with her, I presume?"

"Yes," she replied hesitantly.

"You weren't going to!" María Fernanda said.

"What?"

"If I didn't ask, I wouldn't put it past you not to spend the night with her."

"That's not true, don't you start now . . . The thing is, she doesn't really need it, she's not in that bad of shape."

"Mamá breaks a hip and you say she's not in that bad of shape. So what do you call bad shape, if I may ask?"

They spoke a bit longer, and before hanging up each apologized for their tone, as they always did after arguing, an act that neither added nor solved anything but was a sort of reflex drummed into the women Mamá had raised. Though upset, she wasn't upset enough not to see that neither of them was right to act the way they had, or that being right didn't even matter. The same thing had happened at Christmas, but this time the inability to have a normal conversation with María Fernanda added to her conviction that the weeks to come, until Mamá was released, would be difficult indeed.

Talking to Manuel was like a respite, a break she'd saved until the end. She recounted her mother's condition and the conversations with her siblings as though describing each detail were the only way to find solace. He offered to come along and spend the night at the hospital, but she said no, he should stay with the kids.

"We can call a babysitter, you know it's not a problem."

"No, stay here, I'd rather you be here with them."

It was odd: despite having told Manuel everything, she really hadn't told him anything, which became clear when he asked how she was doing—not her mother but *her*—and she didn't know how to respond.

"I don't know," she said.

"Well, are you upset?"

"I don't know, I don't know how I am."

"Come home after she falls asleep."

When she got back to the hospital, Mamá was on edge.

"Did you call them?"

"Yes."

"What did Antonio say?"

"He's coming tomorrow."

"What did he have to do today?"

"I don't know."

There was a little pause, as though Mamá were waiting to change topics, to provide a ring of silence for what she was about to say.

"You know what today is, don't you?"

"No," she replied, but the second she spoke she knew exactly what day it was, and Mamá must have seen as much in her face because she gave no further explanation.

"God has a real sense of humor," she said finally, as though her words were intended to end all discussion of the matter, behaving more than ever like doña María Antonia, a creature who had changed in recent years, taken on a different disguise, become deceitful. It lasted only a few seconds, for as long as it took to once more impose a ring of silence and then start up with a phony-sounding whimper.

There was no way it could be coincidence. "Ten years?"

"Nine," said Mamá, and the two of them fell silent, as though under orders.

Nine years almost to the minute, since it had been this time of day, or night, when the factory burned down. She recalled almost the entire night, but the images she retained of it, unlike with other memories, were fixed. In particular, she recalled Mamá and Antonio and Joaquín, recalled walking in after having seen the ruins of Alonso Woodworks after the fire, recalled the argument in Mamá's living room, Joaquín claiming—since it was clear that the fire hadn't been accidental—that Antonio was to blame because of the way he ran things, threatening debtors, shouting at employees, making enemies. Having gone to Mamá's to see if her presence might help, she instead felt out of place. Mamá hadn't cried yet, maybe she'd cry later; at the time she looked like a judge.

Antonio, twenty-two at the time, rather than defend himself by challenging anything Joaquín said, simply hurled insults. Not taking her eyes off them, yet somehow looking as though she were hardly paying attention to either one, Mamá got up from her armchair, walked over to Antonio and gave him a resounding slap across the face.

"Go home, son," she said then, not a trace of ire detectable in her tone, as though the slap had been a simple act of justice and his going home the only conceivable thing to do.

Later it occurred to her that it was always the same with people you lived with and were used to; it was like they weren't even there, like they were almost invisible, until suddenly some isolated incident gave them real substance, weight. That was how it was with Antonio, it was as though he hadn't existed until that moment and Mamá's slap had conferred upon him enormous significance. She saw that his pride was wounded less by Mamá herself than by the fact that she'd sided with Joaquín, saw his desperation and, at the same time, his fear, because now that the factory had burned down he was out of a job and didn't even have a degree to fall back on, to help him find something else. All of that—as opposed to the image of her brother about to cry in public for the first time—was what gave texture, weight, smell, to Antonio, who until then had been little more than Antoñito, the baby, who it was almost impossible to have a meaningful conversation with, since he was almost ten years younger. Their talks were monotonous and banal.

But that wasn't the end of the drama. Antonio had left

slowly, with no visible manifestations of rage, but—in that odd way he had—giving the impression that his rancor would never fully heal. And then it was just Mamá, Joaquín, and her left in the room. The silence, interrupted only by Joaquín's obsequious praise of Mamá's stand, seemed to give Mamá space to consider her next move.

"Stand up, sir," she said to Joaquín finally, using the formal *usted*, which was odd, because they used the informal *tú* when speaking to each another.

The slap she gave Joaquín, so unexpected, was almost ridiculous, and he reacted childishly, protesting in vain.

"That's the last time you talk about my son like that."

Joaquín walked out of Mamá's house as the man he'd first been when he arrived at the factory, a small-town rube who wouldn't have had a place to fall down dead had it not been for her. His ridiculous gray suit, overpowering cologne and slicked-back hair turned him back into the man he truly was, then perhaps more than ever.

It struck her then that had Joaquín not left, Mamá would never have realized she was standing there. Her mother sat down in the armchair once more and stared inexpressively, as though no longer wanting to pretend. She felt fear then, a fear that was previous and habitual, so habitual it seemed almost not like fear but like something illogical when applied to her mother: compassion. She'd left home years ago, was married, had a good job, was respected, and yet she didn't know what to do with this compassion she was feeling for her own mother. What a normal person would have

taken as a natural response, to her seemed odd and uncomfortable. In Manuel's family, things weren't complicated.
And if in Manuel's family things weren't complicated, that
meant they didn't have to be. The idea of walking over to
her mother and hugging her crossed her mind, quickly and
painfully, like the blade of a knife.

"What are you doing here?" Mamá asked suddenly.

She couldn't exactly have explained her reaction to those
words. It was as though Mamá had slapped her, too. First
she felt foolish, then she clenched her jaw so that Mamá
couldn't tell. After leaving she nearly turned back, nearly
opened the door and shouted that she was glad the damned
factory had burned down. She cried in the elevator. Not out
of sorrow. Not out of anger, either.

Suddenly everything is slow and senseless. The image of
a silent Mamá, in the hospital bed, blurs with that of the
photo of her in the living room with corkscrew curls, the
two becoming one but without becoming real. She doesn't
love María Fernanda, not really. Antonio is little more than
someone to be pitied for his bad luck, someone discounted
unintentionally, someone to be feared, like a dangerous
breed of dog. Not even Manuel escapes this slowness and,
suddenly, becomes grotesque. With no visible change, for
no logical reason, his tenderness becomes a gentle irritation
that suffocates her, in the same way that her kids—not their
existence but their image, the idea of them, the responsibility they entail—suffocate her.

She recalls the last run-in she had with María Fernanda, in Mamá's kitchen at Christmas that year, the phony joy that always leads into the same conversation about who's gained more weight, recalls her glee on realizing that *she* was thinner, recalls Antonio and Luisa sitting in the living room, not speaking, watching some Christmas show on TV, waiting for dinner, and all of it—the memory and the present—turns into Mamá. She can't stop hating her. It's as if right this moment, on this day and not another that might have been more warranted, she hates Mamá profoundly, utterly, with no hope of forgiveness, as if she holds her solely responsible for this slow motion that makes everything seem so nonsensical, as though a membrane containing her rancor, holding it back, had ruptured and, rather than explode, simply leaked out a liquid contempt, slowly, silently.

"Daughter, it's one tragedy after another," Mamá says, and the words make her jump up, as though she'd been teetering on breaking point, and head for the door.

"Where are you going?"

"I'll be right back."

"Where are you going?"

She made no noise closing the door, made no noise rushing down to the street. It was 1:30 a.m. when the taxi dropped her off at home. She rode up in the elevator, a knot in her throat, as if she were about to cry or to tell a humiliating secret. The kids were asleep. Manuel said, "How are you?" when she walked into the bedroom, but she didn't respond.

"Are you OK?"

Collapsing onto the bed beside him, she got a faint whiff of toothpaste.

"Are you OK?"

She felt ugly beside Manuel and something dark inside her took pleasure in that feeling. She put her hand on his crotch and stroked until she felt him grow excited.

"What's the matter?"

She got on top of him without looking him in the face, with the urge to hurt herself, trying to hurt herself, desperately, as though seeking punishment. Manuel didn't give in easily, first asking why she was doing this and then, writhing away, as if to distance himself from his satisfaction, he stared into her eyes, holding her hair away from her face with one hand. They said nothing more, and the silence intensified the sorrow of Manuel's flesh, sinking into her without understanding her.

But the silence is also this:

Mamá waiting at the hospital.

María Fernanda.

Antonio saying he'll go see Mamá tomorrow, and that it will be hard.

The kids asleep in the next room.

And by virtue of trying to hurt herself she ends up hurting Manuel, who takes on a strange beauty with his pajama bottoms down at his knees, and who—relinquishing his attempts to understand, at least for the time being—pushes her down on the bed, trying for a more standard position that she refuses to grant without knowing why; the only thing she knows is that she has to plumb the depths of this senselessness, to sink into it, and Manuel accepts this, motionless, until finally a dry metallic taste starts in the back of her throat and a fleeting satisfaction descends from far away, a satisfaction which, as she pulls away, seems less a result of physical pleasure than of the familiar beauty of Manuel's erection, the simplicity of his sexuality. It is Manuel whose hands tuck her hair behind her ear, who strokes her cheek, who lies breathing beside her.

"What happened. Tell me."

It started with the smell, the memory of the smell of sanded wood at the factory, rising up from those mounds of shavings piled beside the saws at Alonso Woodworks. María Fernanda would have thought it stupid of her to begin answering Manuel's question this way, but at the moment she found it more logical and coherent than any other answer. And not just the smell. She recalled that when Mamá wasn't around she used to kneel down in one of those mounds of sawdust and sink her hands into it as if it were the warm guts of an animal. She couldn't have been more than ten at the time but still recalled the warm almost sweet smell of the wood, and Joaquín there beside her, looking after her like a well-trained beast, almost fearful, not daring to scold her. Admitting this, she slowly realized, still not looking Manuel full in the face, was like facing up to herself: accepting that not only had she never truly hated the factory but that in fact there was something about it she'd loved dearly; and if that seemed strange now, ridiculous even, it was because deep down it was the opposite: perfectly clear, and significant. Admitting that she'd loved the factory was no different from admitting she'd loved Mamá—not the woman now in the hospital with a broken hip, but doña María Antonia, the one who strode silently among the saws with her tough female authority, Joaquín at her side like an enormous hunting dog. Or maybe not loved her but had at least been seduced by her power, the same power that María Fernanda had so naturally exerted over her throughout their adolescence.

They were, Mamá and María Fernanda, two faces of the same fear. And telling Manuel all of this now was like finding a word that perfectly described a feeling, and, having done so, seeing that reality take on a whole new significance.

"The factory burned down nine years ago today," she said, and Manuel's lips parted, as though he were giving a tiny little involuntary smile.

"Wow," he said.

"I hadn't realized, Mamá told me at the hospital."

"How is she?"

"Bad."

"What did your brother say?"

"That he's going to see her tomorrow."

"I think you should go too."

"Yes."

Saying *yes*, agreeing to Manuel's sensible attitude and at the same time knowing that *she* was the one who'd made the decision was an act that suddenly possessed such simple, everyday beauty that she had the urge to pretend she was still upset, so as to draw the conversation out all night.

"Are you going back to the hospital?"

"I don't know. Do you think I should?"

"I think you need to get a little rest."

"Yes," she said, and seeing Manuel's exhausted face, added, "You're right."

On the other side of the wall, in the room next door, a child coughed.

Her stomachache worsened on walking into the hospital room and the penetrating odor of the hallway, alternating between neutral sterilizer and rancid sweat, followed her in. Mamá was awake.

"I didn't sleep all night," Mamá said immediately, recriminating her for not having stayed. She didn't reply immediately.

"Have you had breakfast yet?" she asked.

"Don't change the subject, don't treat me like an idiot, I'm telling you I didn't sleep all night. I'm your mother." Mamá's apparently unconnected words showed the disjointed thinking of a woman trying to condense into a single sentence what she's been ruminating on all night. "People love their mothers. Or don't your children love you?"

Mamá's brow was drawn, indicating that she was truly in pain, not like the standard performance she put on when she came over and complained to Manuel or the kids, as though convinced that love would automatically follow on from compassion.

"Yes, they do love me."

"Well then. You've never told me that, never once said, 'Mamá, I love you.'"

This was Mamá to a T, or at least Mamá's most ridiculous face. It seemed even more pitiful now, thinness exaggerating her woeful expression, helplessness clearly visible behind the bags under her eyes—helplessness, on a face like hers, that had always had a staunch aristocratic beauty about it. Mamá's melodrama was not only pretense but also the clearest demonstration of her ineptitude, her lack of emotional competence. She asked for love, and if it wasn't forthcoming then she demanded love, and what's more she demanded it like that, the way she would have demanded that her workers re-sand a strip of molding back when the factory was still up and running.

And yet, behind Mamá's thousand faces (or her only one) something was changing, had perhaps already changed, that very night. In the same way that there was a before and after with the factory fire, an after seemed to be created now by Mamá's standard melodramatic reaction that was, nevertheless, somehow different.

* * *

Mamá ate breakfast in silence and with great difficulty, since the brace that had been put on kept her from sitting up; after finishing, she asked what time Antonio had said he'd come.

"I don't know what time, he said today," she replied, fearing that Mamá's questioning would continue.

"He won't come."

"He said he'd come, really."

And she suddenly felt silly, like a little girl who'd told a lie and, on being caught, insisted a thousand times over that it was true.

"He won't come."

Truthfully, given the choice, she herself would have preferred that Antonio not come. Last Christmas had stirred things up more than any time since the fire, and in the end it had solved nothing, leaving them in a state of tension that divided the family into two camps: she and Antonio on one side, as if accepting their victimhood, Mamá and María Fernanda on the other. Though nothing really different had happened that year, they each seemed to feel the overwhelming need to make a stand, and rather than accomplish anything, this only gave the hours-long Christmas dinner a sort of affected, almost grotesque theatricality in which the three of them, pretending it was a normal get-together, each blamed one another for their own unhappiness, albeit never openly. Manuel, the kids, Antonio's wife Luisa, they all seemed mere bit players in this silent confrontation, presided over by Mamá, who finally stood, as she did each year after dessert, and demanded that they sing Christmas carols by the nativity scene she always erected by the front door. Had it not been for the fact that Antonio broke a wineglass against the edge of the table, they might all have gone home with the same sense of assumed failure as they did every other Christmas.

"Time to sing carols," she said, and Antonio shattered the glass decisively. Mamá then tried to cover it up, acting as though it had been an accident, but her fakery—like that of the joyous carols—was suddenly odious.

Antonio and Mamá hadn't spoken since, and the fact that he was now coming to visit made her as uneasy as she had been Christmas day. She suggested turning on the TV so as to fill the silence, and so Mamá would stop complaining, but then regretted it because her mother wanted her to leave it on a channel showing some sort of courtroom reality show. A man who said he had cancer was suing a tobacco company, claiming that when he became addicted there were no health warnings on cigarette packs.

"So," the prosecutor was saying, "you went to your doctor when you noticed the early signs and, as the report states, and he urged you to quit smoking . . ."

Antonio appeared in the doorway looking somber, like someone forced against his will to do something unpleasant, and he was alone, no sign of Luisa, who no doubt would have made things easier. Suddenly it seemed like a planned gathering, and yet without María Fernanda there, Mamá's face took on a vulnerable expression.

"But I was already addicted by that time, you're the ones . . ." the man's voice trembled and the camera, sensing he was about to cry, zoomed in, "to be held responsible for my death, and the deaths of thousands of men and women like me who . . ."

Mamá was no longer watching but Antonio was, as though trying, even now, to escape Mamá.

"Come here, son."

Antonio moved brusquely, banging into a notebook filled with the doctor's notes about meals that was hanging by the door, and kept swaying back and forth with an exasperating clink each time it swung.

"Come here."

It must have been cold out, because Antonio's ears and nose were pink.

"Is a distillery, by chance, held responsible for deaths resulting from drunk drivers?" the prosecutor asked, smoothing his tie. "Is it not, in fact, the consumer's responsibility to make responsible use of the product?"

Though he was thirty-nine years old, standing there before Mamá Antonio looked like a brutish kid who's just had a fight and, finding no way to justify himself, stands in silence. He approached slowly, in a mixture of fear and rancor she didn't recall having seen since the fire, since the night Mamá slapped him in front of Joaquín.

"Would you like it if you were going to die?" the man on TV asked.

"I'm not saying I want you to die, I'm simply saying that it was your responsibility . . ."

Mamá asked for a glass of water. Suddenly the conversation on TV had gotten uncomfortable and she rose too quickly to go and get her mother's water, making obvious what might not have been until then: that she, too, was uncomfortable. When she returned, Mamá drank it down slowly, staring at Antonio the whole time.

"Do you know what cancer is?" The man on TV took off the hat he'd been wearing, revealing a gleaming white, clearly chemo-induced baldness. The audience froze with a timid, "Ohhhh."

"I think things are getting a little overheated here."

"I'm going to die," the man replied. "Does that not justify things getting a little overheated?"

The program, though clearly tragic, though it was true that the man was going to die, contained an element of dramatic posturing that made it sickeningly absurd.

"I'm going to die," the man repeated.

"Do we have to watch this shit?" Antonio asked brusquely, almost shouting without realizing it.

"I don't think it's shit," Mamá responded. "That man is going to die."

It wasn't the fact that he was going to die that made it

sickening, though, it was the fact that he was clearly playing the role of the dying man, the same way Mamá had begun playing—even if her pain was real—the role of the infirm.

"Give me a kiss," Mamá said. "Give your mother a kiss."

Antonio's face froze in a look of shock that gave a whole new meaning to his silence up until that moment. Whether or not Mamá realized what she was asking seemed, by this point, almost irrelevant. Antonio walked over quickly and gave her a peck on the cheek, attempting to disguise how hard it was for him.

"You love me, don't you, son?"

"Do I love you?"

"You love me, don't you?"

And Mamá's question vacillated between pathetic and authoritarian, for despite being insincere, it did not allow *no* for an answer. The *of course* with which Antonio replied was simply the only quick and dignified way out, and they were still in close proximity when the arrival of the doctor suddenly made everything easier, placing them once more in the realms of people feigning ordinary concern. Mamá made no comment when Antonio left after offering an excuse that—given that it was a Sunday—took on a clearly vengeful character: he had to get to work. What she did do, however, was take for granted that *she* would call in to work and take the following day off.

"Tomorrow, before you come in the morning, stop at my house and pick up my other robe, the green one."

"I work tomorrow, Mamá."

"Well, tell them you need the day off. Someone has to

stay with me, don't you think?"

On TV the judge found the tobacco company guilty. The audience applauded feverishly.

She wasn't sure what she was afraid of, but she didn't want to be alone. It may well have been the fact that she'd been unable to keep from siding with Antonio, yet having done so somehow made her feel ashamed. Antonio wasn't completely right either. No one was, really, and when she got home and Manuel asked how things had gone that afternoon, she thought that even he wouldn't understand, even if she recounted everything Mamá had said and the way Antonio had reacted. It all stemmed from things so far in the past, things that had gone unspoken for so many years that there was no way to sum it all up now, to articulate it concretely. And just as it couldn't be explained, nor could it be resolved. It simply was. Her relationship with Mamá, and María Fernanda, and Antonio simply was; it couldn't be described, or altered, or resolved; it rose up before her like a spider's web made of stone, one in which hostilities and hard feelings no longer resembled hostilities or hard feelings but the unsettled scores of people who had given up trying to understand one another, if indeed they had ever tried at all. That was why, when she first met Manuel's family, she got the feeling that their relationships were completely unreal, got the feeling that their love was a sham even more elaborate than that of her own family. Discovering later that their affection was genuine turned her against Mamá in a subtle way, because in the same sense that Manuel's mother had been solely responsible for the love in his family, Mamá must have been to blame for the distance and envy in hers.

The needy way she loved Manuel's mother resembled that of an orphan trying too hard to please her adoptive parents, to the point of coming off as ridiculous, and every time she thought about her mother-in-law (now that the woman was dead), she got the almost comforting urge to cry, recalling how quiet and kindhearted she'd been, how tiny. There was no sense fooling herself, either: no matter how she'd tried to make her own family resemble Manuel's, Mamá's overbearing shadow always triumphed in the end. Since she and Manuel lived far away, Mamá, since the fire, had taken to spending the entire weekend with them, to be with Manuel and the kids. If she had ever been given the chance to reproach Mamá, it wouldn't be for coming over but for doing so the way she did—condescendingly, with no sign of gratitude, as though looking down on someone simply doing their duty out of a sense of obligation. She refrained from bickering with her mother, because doing so always made her feel cruel, and because she didn't want Manuel to realize how on edge she was. Mamá could be very convincing, and being upset made her behave abruptly, so whenever there was an argument she ended up feeling her mother had won, and consoled herself by believing that everyone takes silent revenge, and this was hers: offering Mamá her home, but not her affection. Which was why, when she got back from the hospital that night, she took down the photo

. Mamá had put in the living room, because it was her silent revenge, and she could no longer stand her corkscrew curls, her black-and-white photo-studio smile, aged twenty. Then she called the office and said she wouldn't be able to come in the following day, that her mother's condition was serious and she needed to be there for her.

María Fernanda always looked the same in pictures: same open smile, same shiny hair, exact same expression in her eyes. Seeing her grow up, in successive photo albums, was like viewing an art exhibit about the passage of time on a beautiful and immutable face that, despite undergoing no structural change, seemed to wither ever so slightly with each passing second. Sometimes she thought that if María Fernanda hadn't been so aware of her own beauty, it would have been impossible to feel anything but proud to be her sister, in much the same way that she enjoyed being Manuel's wife, though it relegated her to a sort of secondary status. If she'd been envious, it was never of María Fernanda's beauty but of her self-assurance, of her ability to adapt to any environment, any conversation. And if liking things about her sister that she often disliked about her mother was contradictory, she wasn't too concerned about it, just as she wasn't too concerned about the fact that it was Monday and she was using up vacation days to look after Mamá. It would be awhile before Antonio returned to the hospital, and María Fernanda, with her constant phone calls from Valencia, did nothing but get Mamá worked up, make her complain about how uncomfortable the hospital room was rather than accept it, which would have made the whole thing less of a struggle.

Later, she called the school where Manuel taught and listed the facts:

1. Mamá looked worse.

2. The doctor was talking about some sort of complication with her digestive system.

3. She'd had broth and yogurt for lunch.

4. There was no news from Antonio.

5. Mamá's caretaker had left a message saying Joaquín called.

She made an effort to describe the facts, to explain them as clearly as possible to Manuel, as though this might shed light on her peculiar reactions to them, or on the fear that she again felt at being in the hospital, or on the utterly astonished feeling she—who had always considered herself a victim of Mamá—got by contemplating the possibility that perhaps Mamá hadn't been so uncaring, that perhaps she herself was more to blame than she'd thought; and she tried to examine the thornier world of her rancor, struggling to identify concrete facts that could justify her inability to forgive her mother. She saw, then, that even the times when she'd most clearly found Mamá to blame, there shone a tiny glimmer of doubt that suddenly turned against her, made her all the things she'd never wanted to be: unfair, cynical, judgmental, incapable of understanding; the image of

Mamá changing ("The fracture could lead to a progressive, more generalized degeneration of the whole organism," the doctor had said), fighting for her ("we've noticed a few reactions"), becoming if not lovable then at least comprehensible ("not necessarily related to the fracture that reveal a deterioration of other organs"); and the worst thing was, maybe it was only the fact that the doctor had spoken this way, in the grave tones of a man not discounting the possibility of a quick demise, that forced her to face the logical—and yet absolutely absurd—fact that Mamá, like every human being, would one day die.

She bought magazines in order to conceal her bafflement, to hide it, if possible, behind the frivolous sorts of comments that had always gotten a rise from Mamá, and although the strategy worked that afternoon, there was a notable phoniness to her chatter, one that in any other situation she would have called fear, but now had no idea what to call it.

"Antonio looks like Papá, don't you think?"

Her question was only part of the real question, the easiest part, and Mamá, who seemed to have been open to this veiled conversation all day, closed down ("Sometimes"), as though wanting to believe she had more time, as though reserving a longer response for later ("But only sometimes").

For as easy as it was to talk about María Fernanda, it was just as difficult to talk about Antonio, or Papá. Papá, always the memory of his funeral that didn't seem like a memory, always the image of the charcoal portrait of him in the living room, in the factory office, but the conversation never went beyond his flat forehead, which Antonio had inherited, or his meek inept expression, which Antonio had inherited, because whenever she asked about him, Mamá responded with a superficial portrait that seemed more like some folksy nineteenth-century novel than an honest description of who he'd been: an unnecessary man.

That was why she didn't mention that Joaquín had called. Telling her mother would have been a new victory for Mamá, perhaps the only one she'd taken seriously since the factory burned down. Joaquín having asked for severance pay after the fire, and Mamá having fired him without any (a symbolic gesture that she knew from the start would cost her dearly) were things that had disheartened Mamá the same way a woman is disheartened by contemplating the arrogance of her spoiled child, and although in the end Joaquín got his money, he paid for it with his reputation after attempting to set up his own business using Alonso Woodworks' customers.

The only truly cruel thing Mamá had done, the one time she herself might admit to being deliberately cruel, was to wait for Joaquín to invest all of his money and then destroy him, and since all it took was a couple of phone calls, she did it over a space of time and so subtly that not even Joaquín himself could understand how he went bankrupt. Mamá was clean and unerring, and simple—the definition of a perfect crime—but in order to seal her victory she needed Joaquín's repentance, needed to have him at her feet once more, like a dog that returns home starving after having tried unsuccessfully to run away.

Not telling her that Joaquín had phoned was also the ultimate proof that, even after admitting that Mamá's neglect might not have been entirely voluntary, she wasn't so easily going to let herself be beaten by this sudden pity for her mother, this desire to offer forgiveness when her mother hadn't even asked to be forgiven yet.

"It may be more than a complication, it may be more generalized," the doctor had said, laying new ground, using a completely different tone than he had on the first day, his *may* nothing like the initial, sure-sounding "it will be a slow recovery," and not telling Mamá anything about the doctor's assessment, either, now left her in a privileged position, like someone watching a blind man stride confidently toward a wall and doing nothing to stop him.

Twenty-two years ago she and María Fernanda slept in the same room. It seemed absurd to think of that now, but in fact it wasn't, because something in Mamá's expression had merged them—Mamá and her sister—had turned them into a single perception, simpler, more concrete. On the wall by the top of her bed, María Fernanda had put up a photo of Kirk Douglas, in *Ulysses*, half-naked, in underwear that looked more like a rag, about to take on someone much bigger than him and looking as though he were going to ravish him rather than punch him; and she'd hung it there because she was crazy about Kirk Douglas, crazy in particular about the dimple in his chin, his rugged face, so like the rugged face of that boy from Somontes who was a skeet shooter, the one she'd slept with; and after María Fernanda had told her about it she'd imagined her sister, legs spread, in such detail that she couldn't help but feel revolted by María Fernanda's sexuality, and also by the goofy expression Papá always had in photographs, where he was never touching Mamá ("It's impossible to predict the reactions an elderly person's body might have in these circumstances," the doctor had said). Deep down they weren't so different, not even now that María Fernanda had gained weight and Mamá was so hollow and pasty, her skin like beige clay. If she'd initially feared introducing Manuel to María Fernanda, it was not only out of insecurity but also out of fear that he might be captivated by her sexuality. Mamá allowed María Fernanda to wear the kind of skirts she herself was hardly even allowed to try on, with the sorry excuse that there was "a right way to wear them" and while María Fernanda looked natural in them, she looked like she was about to go street-walking ("A hooker, that's what you look like"), and this comment, made in the cruel tones Mamá often used when returning from the factory, was enough to dissuade her. But not only did Manuel not fall at her sister's feet, he hardly even noticed her, and this was the first and best victory she'd had over María Fernanda: a man, finally, had chosen her. The fact that it took some time to establish their intimacy, physically, didn't matter to him, once she stopped worrying about Manuel's sexuality. In the car—it didn't matter if it was late but they did have to be someplace secluded—she could feel his hand slip through the undone buttons of her blouse, resting lightly on her chest ("Indeed, this deterioration could be related to her arthritis," the doctor had said) or his fingers slip beneath her bra, but more often not, without wanting to take off her clothes, because she felt more at ease being sexual with clothes on, Manuel's pants getting a wet spot, him smiling and opening the windows to clear the steam; and this was no doubt more comfortable than María Fernanda's sexual acrobatics with the champion skeet shooter from Somontes who looked just like Kirk Douglas taking aim, his rugged face just the same, his cleft chin just the same, the same boy who, when María Fernanda broke up with him, came calling day and night like a lost little lamb, like a hunting dog, like Joaquín striding into the dining room on Sundays back when the factory was still in business, saying, "María Antonia, we have to deal with the saw contractor," and her mother replying, "Later, Joaquín," and him taking slow satisfied sips of his wine as though he'd just wanted to prove he could speak to her so informally—not to the woman now writhing from hip pain ("It's one tragedy after another") but doña María Antonia, the woman who died nine years ago when the factory burned down and left in her place, in her bones, this other woman who'd inherited only the silent desire to know everything about everyone, the desire to control everyone.

She went home for dinner, making the most of Mamá having dozed off. When she walked in Manuel was giving the kids their dinner, and the ordinariness of the scene seemed almost ridiculous compared to the intensity of what she'd been ruminating on all day.

"How's it going?" he asked.

"OK."

"Your brother called. He sounded on edge. Did something happen?"

"No. What did he say?"

"For you to call him. Are you sure everything's OK?"

"Yes."

Antonio was home; Luisa answered and passed the phone to him immediately, cautiously, treating it as an important call.

"What the fuck was all that yesterday?" Antonio barked with the brusqueness other people's reactions always brought out in him.

"All what?"

"What do you mean *all what*? That scene Mamá made. What the hell's the matter with you?"

"Don't speak to me that way, Antonio."

"I'm sorry."

She couldn't pretend the conversation was not, on some level, satisfying. It essentially revealed that she, the big sister, was the only authority figure Antonio recognized.

"You know how Mamá thinks of us: you're the failure and I'm the dimwit."

"So what was she trying to do?"

"Prove it to you, prove it to both of us, I suppose."

Admitting this so openly tinged her words with a sort of fearfulness that made Manuel look up. He hadn't stopped watching her since the conversation started, and the kids were fussing, perhaps surprised at this unjustified interruption to their dinner.

"But why? Why prove it to us?"

"I think she's dying, Antonio, and what's worse: I think she's perfectly aware of the fact that she's dying. She's acting really weird: she hardly spoke at all today, and she's so pale; I think she's dying."

She'd poured all this out so quickly that Manuel hardly had time to react. Nor did Antonio, and suddenly it seemed fake: the words she's used, Manuel's expression, Antonio's silence; it was as though it were impossible to discuss death without turning it into a performance, an affectation.

"Did the doctor say something to you?"

"The doctor just makes these comments, you know, like he's washing his hands of the whole thing. He says her condition may deteriorate progressively."

"What's she saying?" Luisa whispered, barely audible, from behind Antonio.

"Shh, I'll tell you in a minute," he replied. And then, "Are you going back tomorrow?"

"Yes."

"María Fernanda has to be told."

That was Antonio's classic way of saying he wasn't going to be the one to do it.

"I'll tell her, I'll call her from the hospital tomorrow."

"She called this afternoon," Manuel said, guessing at their conversation.

"What did she say?"

"That she'd call back later."

"I'll take care of it," she said, addressing Antonio again, "I'll call her tomorrow."

"OK."

And they hung up. Manuel's look suddenly made her uncomfortable.

"How do you feel?" he asked.

"I don't know," she replied. "I have no idea."

Fear. Fear that they'd be mentally or physically disabled, or ugly, or too fat; and nightmares, she had nightmares in which, from the moment she found out they were going to be twins, she pictured them joined at the back, forced to wave a single arm or kick a single leg, offspring whose ugliness was like her, but a grotesque version. Now they were three and it seemed idiotic to have thought those things, but at the time, starting halfway through the pregnancy, her age, and all those years on the pill, and all those women's magazines, had made her feel petrified and almost entirely certain that something horrific would be wrong with the kids. Mamá became a grandmother without so much as conceding that her fears were not wholly groundless, without even understanding, really, that the reason she'd waited so long to become a mother was because she wanted to prove something, to show that—like María Fernanda—she too could have a professional life. There came a moment when she thought that Mamá actually cared more about being named godmother at the baptism than about the fact that they'd been born, and it made her so sick that she was on the verge of asking some random girlfriend to be their godmother instead.

In the end, it was Mamá, of course, but Manuel had had to do everything he could to calm her down so that her hostility wouldn't be evident throughout the ceremony. And then afterward she was afraid, absurdly and unjustifiably afraid—like she was now, after having spoken to María Fernanda—about having more or less argued with her mother.

Sex with Manuel did nothing for her that night, but she needed it, in a compulsive sort of way. It was, in fact, a dodge, something she pounced on knowing that it wouldn't make her feel any better but also that it would make the night pass more quickly. And then afterward she returned to the hospital, because she didn't want to stay with Manuel, either: staying would have meant having to explain too many things.

Walking out, she got the strange sense that she was abandoning them, and all the words she hadn't said to María Fernanda began to fill her throat. As always, after arguing with her sister, being upset filled her with uneasiness and made her feel impotent, made her pore over their exchange, searching for the words she should have said, for comebacks that would have hit the mark, and also made her regret what she actually had said. And because she went through this same routine every time, her sense of failure was like a familiar story, one repeated since adolescence.

Mamá was asleep when she arrived but awoke from the sound the armchair made, as she sat down beside the bed.

"Where have you been?"

"At home. I went back to feed the kids," she lied.

"Ah."

Mamá's mouth was dry, which made her look even more pitiful, so she went into the tiny bathroom and came back with a glass of water, which her mother drank quickly and also, since she couldn't sit up very well, spilled onto her nightgown. Her lips trembled theatrically.

"I want you to get me out of here," she said.

"Get you out of here? Where do you want to go? You're not in good shape, Mamá, the doctors need to see you, you're in no state to go home."

She'd adopted that phony tone again, as though speaking to a little girl, trying to talk her out of some ridiculous whim, but Mamá's tragic tone had been no more natural.

"I'm not talking about going home. I want to go to another hospital, a private hospital, the doctors here are killing me."

"For God's sake, nobody's killing you."

"I want to leave."

"You don't have the money, Mamá."

She said it knowing how cruel those words would sound to her mother, but they didn't produce the effect she'd hoped for, the normal one, the grimace of disgust people made when confronted with some trivial, impulsive peccadillo they've committed; instead she gave an intent serious look, one that seemed to have predicted her daughter's response and now almost delighted in having been right.

"I want that million," she replied, looking her in the eyes.

"What million?"

"The million pesetas I gave you and Manuel for the house."

"That was fifteen years ago, Mamá."

"I want it back."

She remembered the money perfectly, of course, because over the years it had been one of Mamá's favorite bones to pick, a specter that made stormy appearances, often after arguments, one that made even Manuel, who was generally so laidback, so angry that he'd refuse to speak to Mamá. And now it had appeared again, this time with a seriousness that bore not the hallmark tone people used when bringing up a favor they've granted as the prelude to a request but the intransigence of a legal summons.

"I don't have it, you know perfectly well that I'm drowning in bills and paperwork."

Those words were the only way she could find to ask for clemency, though she saw immediately that forgiveness would not be easily granted.

"If you loved me you'd give me the money, if you really loved me you couldn't stand seeing me in this piece of shit hospital."

The fact that it was nighttime actually made it easier to see what Mamá was really saying: this was a debt that could never be repaid because this debt was a sort of ultimatum on love, or the only way Mamá could conceive love.

"I'd have to apply for a loan, refinance the house," she said quietly, as though talking to herself, because she knew that, rather than make Mamá reconsider, this would only reaffirm her mother's sense of importance. Mamá exchanged her serious face for her vulnerable one, her entreaty face that was absolutely insufferable, as insufferable as the suddenly overpowering old-lady smell, as insufferable as the sound of Mamá's tongue against the roof of her mouth as she swallowed saliva.

"María Fernanda is coming tomorrow," she told her mother. "I called her today."

But not even that made Mamá react.

"You're going to give me the money, aren't you, daughter?"

Again the smell. Again the revulsion rising in her throat, making her crack her knuckles anxiously.

"Do you know what it would take for me to get you a million pesetas, Mamá? Do you realize what I'd have to do—do you?"

She'd shouted without intending to, she realized on falling silent, and immediately the sound of a hospital attendant's footsteps could be heard heading for the room.

"You're going to give it to me, aren't you, daughter?"

"Yes, Mamá, I'm going to give it to you, this is going to be the last thing I give you."

"I'm asking for what's mine."

"And I'm giving it to you, but shut up already."

"You don't know what I went through, to send you and your brother and sister to the best schools."

"Shut up!"

The attendant rushed in and brusquely instructed her to leave. Mamá had started to cry and was speaking in the histrionic tones of a woman accustomed to feigning an emotion she's never felt.

"Mothers should be loved and respected, don't you think?" Mamá asked the attendant silently glaring at her in reproach, as though she were a criminal. "They should be loved and respected."

"Of course they should, Señora, now don't get yourself all worked up."

"All I was asking for is the money that's mine—and love, that's what I was asking for, love."

When Mamá said that, she stopped arguing with the

attendant, who was shoving her out of the room, and ran down the hall to get out of there as quickly as possible. She arrived home sweating. Manuel was asleep.

It's not the idea of death in general but the reality of Mamá's death that seems so absurd. María Fernanda is probably already at the hospital. She'll have spoken to the doctor. She'll have told Mamá the truth. Although it's cold out, the sky is clear and Mamá will have seen it from her bed and then turned to María Fernanda and cried, maybe.

You tell a woman that she's going to die, you say, "You're going to die," and it makes no difference if you do it slowly, or lovingly, or if you hold her hand; you say, "You're going to die"—something she herself had been aware of all her life and even reflected on deeply, more than once, as though she herself were seventy years old—and it's like hearing a door slam, like when Manuel's mother stopped after being told "You're going to die" and looked at her, not at Manuel or his brother or his brother's children but at her, over by the door, standing far from the bed out of pure embarrassment, as though trying to escape the performance that would have been required by standing with them, the one impossible for her to feign in the four or five seconds during which her face froze in an idiotic expression ("You're going to die") that more resembled a smile.

That's why she's not at all surprised when María Fernanda asks, from the hospital, why she didn't tell Mamá the truth about the state of her health. She's not up to arguing with María Fernanda. She's too tired, she hardly slept all night.

And she shouldn't have reacted that way about the money, either, or didn't she realize Mamá was only asking for what was hers?

"I know," she replied, hoping her sister would be quiet. "Look, tell Mamá that Manuel went to the bank to apply for a loan this morning and she'll have her million in no time."

Was she going to the hospital later, after work?

"No, I'm not; you're already there, why do I need to go?"

That wasn't the point, what on earth was the matter with her, María Fernanda was tired too, for goodness sake, not only did she have a fever but she'd come in all the way from Valencia.

"What do you want me to say?"

Nothing, or at least not to *her*, but she should at the very least go to the hospital to apologize to Mamá, she owed her that much, and so did Antonio; she should call and tell him to go that evening as well.

"Why don't you call him?"

She knew perfectly well why.

"No, I don't."

Stop playing dumb, she knew perfectly well that Antonio didn't want to speak to her.

"What makes you so sure? Have you ever tried?"

In the end, she caved, agreeing to both things: she'd phone Antonio and she'd go to the hospital after work. Manuel called from the bank to ask for her national ID number, which he needed for the loan application. The babysitter called to say that one of the twins had a fever and the other was misbehaving like she wouldn't believe: he'd broken the little clown figurine on the counter and she'd spanked him. María Fernanda called again. Antonio said he didn't know if he'd go or not, he had to think about it. Mamá's caretaker phoned with another message about Joaquín having called. Manuel called to say the loan had been approved. Her boss asked if she was planning to spend all day on the family helpline. She spilled coffee on a report. She went into the bathroom to cry, and a colleague in there gave her a hug, saying she was there for her, whenever or whatever, because she knew how hard it was to see your mother die, how incredibly painful it was to see your mother die.

Leaving the office, she thought that if it had been a less beautiful day, colder at least, everything would have been easier, and was shocked at her own detachment, at how little she cared that Mamá was dying, at how indifferent she was to María Fernanda's grievances and Antonio's pain.

When she got home, Manuel said that her sister had called twice to tell her not to go to the hospital, that her mother was being moved to a private clinic that same afternoon. She cried again, just so that Manuel would hold her. He smelled of cigarettes, and mint.

"Do you want me to go with you?"

"No."

"Want me to drive you and wait in the car while you go up to see her?"

"What about the kids?"

"They can stay with the neighbor, I already spoke to her."

Manuel's love was so warm, so simple. She wished she could surrender to it like a girl awaiting supreme, logical guidance. She wished she could say, "Tell me what to do, how to act." In the car they spoke only of the loan, its terms. Three years. They could swing it, but there would be no vacation in August, unless of course her mother—and here Manuel paused, as though this were a territory best left untrodden . . .

"I want no part of my mother's money, the last thing in the world I want is my mother's money, do you understand me?"

"Of course," Manuel said.

All three of them were there, and had it not been for María Fernanda the silence would have been more difficult than ever. None of them looked directly at the other for longer than necessary, and when they spoke they did so addressing Mamá—not her face but her hands, or the outline of her knees under the sheet. Mamá stank. She could recall no sharper or more unpleasant smell, and it remained lodged in her brain even after she left the room. Mamá looked notably worse than the day before. The doctors said it was due to the move, and to the incompetence of whoever had put on her brace incorrectly, not tightening it properly. The pain she was feeling now was for her own good, the doctor repeated tirelessly, each time he walked into the room, as though what was making her purse her lips in a perpetual grimace might be an unnecessary form of torture. The room was understatedly pleasant, like a classy hotel, and yet couldn't escape the cold anonymity of a hospital. The little touches to be expected at a private clinic—the delicate vase containing a single rose, the curtains—only served to highlight Mamá's helplessness, accentuate it to the point that her pain looked so ugly it was grotesque. María Fernanda addressed only her, even when she was actually speaking to Antonio; and Antonio, who arrived later, looking like an interchangeable extra, did not alter his expression once all evening, wearing the timid-brute face so characteristic of his anxiety.

Mamá slept late and they took advantage of this in order to speak to the doctor, who couldn't keep from adopting a scientific tone—surely an automatic defense mechanism—to speak of Mamá's deteriorating condition.

"How long," Antonio said, abruptly cutting the doctor off, his intonation in no way resembling that of a question.

"Do you mean how long does she have to live?" the doctor asked.

"Yes."

"I can't believe how crude you are," María Antonio replied, looking straight at Antonio for the first time.

"I can't believe what a hypocrite you are."

"Who do you think you are, speaking to me like that?"

Forced to choose, she'd take Antonio's brusqueness over the pretend scandalized tone María Fernanda adopted as a means of avoiding the conversation that, if they were honest, would have to be had sooner or later.

"How long does she have?" she asked, stepping in to end the conversation as quickly as possible, and to quell the doctor's discomfort.

"Her deterioration is progressing, quickly. The change has been dramatic since she arrived. But you can never predict these things with any certainty. It could be a month, maybe less. Essentially, it's up to her."

The doctor, who was so young he'd yet to master the skill of dissembling, must have thought that they were fighting over money. The truth, as almost always, was much more complicated and something that not even they could have explained. The sum total of Mamá's assets, once split three ways, was relatively paltry, but they hadn't gathered around Mamá's deathbed out of love or concern either, so it seemed hard not to accept that they were some sort of spectators. Though the idea would have been morbid had it been anyone else, because this was Mamá it was not. It was as though the three of them saw themselves as exclusive spectators, the sole ticket-holders in a three-seat amphitheater on whose stage Mamá was acting out her own death, with the solemnity of something both longed for and not, by turns both grotesque and pitifully touching. María Fernanda took revenge on Antonio by not bothering to look at him when the two of them later argued over whether or not they should tell Mamá. She was the only one who didn't think they should, who thought it better to wait until closer to the time, and despite claiming that this was in order not to worry Mamá, deep down she was afraid of her reaction to learning how near she was to death.

Since Antonio sided with her, they decided to hold off, to wait at least five days, see if she improved and decide then. But the following day when she went to the hospital after work, it was clear that María Fernanda had already told her everything. She could tell even before her mother spoke, by the rarified silence in the room, by Mamá's look, which suddenly bore into her with severity, as though she were a traitor.

"Would you like it if you were going to die and no one told you, daughter?" Mamá asked unnecessarily.

"Yes," she replied, feeling sincere for the first time. "I think I'd prefer not to be told."

"It's clear that I am not you."

María Fernanda didn't look at her then, or during the half-hour monologue Mamá gave that, as always, excluded the two of them, a monologue to which the reality of death lent a strange detachment. Death, which at first was entirely real, the great truth, seemed to distance her from the woman she'd been all her life; Mamá seemed now less likely than ever to die, it was as though the news of her death had somehow revitalized her.

María Fernanda took the train back to Valencia that night. And if they barely said goodbye, it was because some part of her sister suddenly seemed to acknowledge the toll that telling Mamá had taken. María Fernanda had always been like that, but now, finally, seemed to see it. Her sister was strolling out the door, having fulfilled the expectations of the noble daughter, and leaving *her* with the problem.

Her sister had gotten fatter, and uglier. Exhaustion had reddened her eyelids and made her cheekbones look shiny and uneven, slack. She saw María Fernanda's ugliness as a triumph almost greater even than her remorse. The act of forgiveness (even if María Fernanda had cried, admitted she was wrong) didn't add anything, really. What was truly significant was not Mamá's melodramatic speech—almost nineteenth-century in tone and absurdly well-delivered—about the honest daughter and the insincere daughter and death and how hard she'd worked all her life only to be treated like this, but the fact that at this precise moment, María Fernanda was, truly and objectively, uglier than she was. Forgiveness, if silence counted as forgiveness, was a way of avoiding another truth, one that said true salvation came not from granting forgiveness but from asking for it. That sense of satisfaction, which later made her feel strangely afraid, seemed in fact to express a dissatisfaction with the situation; she almost would have preferred to be the one who asked María Fernanda for forgiveness, because that would have made victory resounding and absolute. And nevertheless it was true that Mamá was dying, just as it was true that Antonio wouldn't forgive Mamá nor would Mamá forgive Antonio, and that each of them could enumerate

their resentments perfectly, with facts and dates that justified them but didn't make them right.

María Fernanda left, defeated, at 9:35, with just enough
time to catch the last train, as though running out of time
were another way to ask forgiveness. Mamá, once they were
alone again, glared as though at a friend whose duplicity has
been discovered.

Manuel wasn't distancing himself. Or if he was, it was only
unconsciously, speaking about the loan they'd taken out,
which, under the terms they'd selected would take three
years to pay off. And yet listening to him talk about money
in this serious tone, so unlike Manuel, was oddly familiar,
reminiscent of her adolescence, of meals at which Joaquín
would report ploddingly and meticulously on the factory,
with the fastidiousness of a bumpkin re-counting his pile of
coins a hundred times just to be sure. Perhaps that was why
all night she felt she was having a realization, seeing that
she'd wasted too much time running in circles on an absurd
track, continuously passing the truth without seeing it. And
the truth was suddenly, again, the factory, but now like a
living being, another member of the family, the favorite
child maybe, one whose life or death or memory was no
different to Mamá than that of a human being. The factory
was like a thirty-year old river running through her life, one
whose course had determined her mother's joy and sorrow
and which, even now that it no longer existed, in some way
continued to determine it. All deaths leave one or two things

in their wake, things they touched whose mere presence becomes suddenly symbolic, as if death's final act were to empty every living thing around and then fill it back up with itself, giving it new meaning. Something like that must have happened with Mamá's feelings about Joaquín and Antonio after the factory burned down. The fact that one of them was her son must have been like finding a kindly person insufferable, someone you feel a desperate, vexatious urge to get away from. It wasn't that she saw Antonio as a failure, but that she saw him as responsible for her failure and as symbolic of the factory. That was why Mamá showed no interest in the money Antonio made by renting out the property where Alonso Woodworks had stood and yet was insisting that *she* pay back the million pesetas associated with her memory of wealth. It wasn't money itself Mamá really wanted, it was money that reminded her of the factory office, the enormous table and matching writing desk; what she wanted was actually her sense of financial security, and for any reminder of her failure to be hidden, in as dignified a way as possible. That was why the hospital room curtains, the elegant armchair for visitors, the rose blossoming in its little vase—beautiful and yet anonymous, like the elegance of a luxury hotel—were more Mamá than Mamá herself.

The entire world was nothing but smell the next day in the hospital room, and Mamá was this: a creature who was herself for a few hours, in the early morning, and then, when the Nolotil-induced torpor wore off, began to emit a sharp animal-like wail whose volume increased until it morphed into something that resembled a cry even though it wasn't, really, and since this quickly dried out her tongue, it left her unable to speak. It was as though Mamá, after María Fernanda had left the previous night, crossed some thin wall, a point of no return. For a few minutes she was almost certain Mamá was about to die. It was during what seemed like a respite, after one of her prolonged monotone wails, which ended, rather than in a respite, in agitated breath-holding. She became afraid. She, who hadn't feared her mother's death until that moment, who couldn't honestly have said that any of her feelings about it had resembled fear, suddenly felt herself slip and fall into the gaping abyss of Mamá's wide-open eyes. Only her eyes. The rest of her body remained contracted in pain, still subject to what seemed more phony than ever, phony the way Mamá's pain always seemed, Mamá's moaning, Mamá's love, Mamá's concern, all of it phony except for her wide-open eyes, hard as knuckles, perhaps begging for clemency. She shouted, "Doctor." She recalls having shouted the word "Doctor" several times, loud, and also having shouted "Mamá," and then "Doctor" again. She recalls having shouted perhaps not so they would save Mamá but save her from Mamá, so there would be another body present to save her from the absurdity, the horrifically real absurdity, the brutal absurdity of death appearing before her. The doctor rushed in and brusquely pushed her aside. The nurse did too. She gazed at Mamá's knees, nearly invisible beneath the sheets.

She thought later, in the hours that followed, that worse than the piercing, almost theatrical apparition of death was the grave silence that followed, the silence in which it no longer even mattered whether or not she forgave Mamá. Life, which had seemed immense, was suddenly miniscule and insignificant, hardly even deserved to be spoken. Although perhaps rather than life, it was death that didn't deserve to be spoken, the way that in death two people as different as Manuel's mother and Mamá adopted the same gestures, the same expressions. The reason they'd seemed so moving on one and so grotesque on the other turned out to have nothing to do with the gestures themselves but the way in which *she*, as spectator, interpreted them, and she saw that now, realized that precisely what repulsed her about Mamá had moved her when it was Manuel's mother. No, she no longer felt hatred ("We can administer morphine," the doctor had said), what she felt now was harder to interpret than hate: María Fernanda, perhaps, aged twenty-two, standing up to Mamá, announcing that she was taking a job in Valencia, going to live in Valencia, "Alone," Mamá had said, and María Fernanda had replied, "No, with Pedro," back when Pedro was just a student, had just graduated with a degree in medicine; "You're not going," Mamá had said, and her sister had replied, "Yes, I am; I'm leaving tomorrow," "Over my dead body," "Over your dead body," which, in fact, was what had made her proud of her sister, her staunch resolution, later expressed in letters detailing how happy she was, with slight condescension toward her dimwit of a sister, toward her failure of a brother. Mamá saying, "I know where she got that grit, and it's not from her father, that's for sure," ("This morning's attack affected a large part of her nervous system," the doctor had said) and she'd sat in the dining room, vaguely unwilling to get up, the manly smell of Joaquín's cologne, his slicked-back hair, his country walk made more pronounced by the tasteful suits Mamá picked out for him. No, it no longer made any difference whether or not she forgave Mamá, and the only reason she called Antonio was because that was what she was supposed to do after what had happened that morning, to tell him that Mamá had asked for a priest—Mamá, a priest ("The morphine will relieve most of her pain, but she might become incredibly sleepy, perhaps delirious," the doctor had said). If they decided to administer morphine maybe he should come see her first, and the priest was coming that very afternoon so they should probably tell María Fernanda to come back too.

The priest is young and handsome. So beautiful in fact that it's almost indecent, almost morbid. He arrives late but approaches Mamá tenderly, and it is his lack of guile that saves him. Each second, when it arrives, is ancient, each feeling experienced. He asks the doctor her name, and before walking out the doctor replies, "María Antonia."

"María Antonia Alonso," Mamá says.

"María Antonia, are you ready to confess?" the priest asks.

"I have nothing to confess, I called you here to bless me."

"We all have something to confess," the young priest replies, his perplexity overly apparent. "The Lord says even the just man sins seven times a day."

"I have no interest in what the just man does," Mamá responds. "As that other man said, 'I fought the good fight and now I want my crown.'"

"That's not exactly what Paul says; he says, 'I have fought the good fight, I have finished the race, I have kept the faith. Now there is *in store for me* the crown of righteousness.'"

The young priest's exactitude irks Mamá and she thrashes in her bed.

"Right, I want my crown."

"'In store for me,' Paul says."

"Same thing."

There comes a brief silence in which suddenly life is crueler than it is absurd, in which Mamá becomes María Antonia Alonso, back at the factory once more, shouting at Joaquín over the phone, telling him to have them re-do the frames, until they've been sanded properly.

"I have nothing to repent," Mamá claims again, "I'm only asking for what's mine, just what's mine, that's all I ask," and then looks at her, the unpardonable traitor, adding, "and love, I'm asking for love."

The priest has picked up on her disgust at Mamá's last words and looks at her longer than necessary. She once again feels the weight of Mamá, the phony way she crosses herself, and thinks, *You never loved me; repent.* The priest places an altar cloth on the bed, beside Mamá, and a host wafer that he treats with delicate, almost ridiculous tenderness. Then he opens his missal and recites:

"I commend you, dear sister María Antonia, to almighty God, and entrust you to your Creator. May you return to Him who formed you, from the dust of the earth."

Mamá glances over but looks away instantly, disgusted, as though she were a leper, and closes her eyes. Suddenly it was as if Mamá had no hands or feet, as though her faux-religiosity were to blame for their atheism—hers and María Fernanda's and Antonio's. She thinks that if Mamá has just one sincere reaction to the priest's words, it will be enough to save her, to purify her entirely, and then she can forgive her.

"When your soul shall depart from your body, may the resplendent multitude of angels meet you. May the court of the apostles receive you. May the triumphant army of glorious martyrs come out to welcome you. May the splendid company of confessors clad in their white robes encompass you. May the choir of joyful virgins receive you. And may you meet with a blessed repose in the bosom of the patriarchs."

But the light from Mamá's eyes is still obsessive, accusing, and she suddenly thinks that her mother's life is not determined by this smile she now contemplates, the smile of a dying woman receiving a tribute she feels is deserved. And she loves her mother, now, the way you love a girl who is stupid and selfish, but has nevertheless received a punishment greater than the one she deserved.

"Far from you be all the terror of darkness, the hiss of flames, the anguish of torment. Far from you be the accursed Satan and his accomplices. Let him shrink abashed into the vast chaos of everlasting night when you draw near with your escort of angels."

"Amen," Mamá says, and Antonio walks in awkwardly, stopping short in the doorframe at this shocking tableau. The priest pauses, marking his place in the missal with a finger, and looks up at him. Perhaps Antonio is thinking, *You never loved me; repent.* Life, made more ridiculous by the presence of the hospital window, is the sound of a bus horn.

"May Christ, Son of the living God, give you a place in the ever verdant gardens of His Paradise and may He, the true shepherd, own you for one of His flock. May you see your Redeemer face to face, and standing ever in His presence gaze with delighted eyes on Truth itself made manifest. There take your place in the ranks of the blessed, and enjoy the blessed vision of your God forever."

"Amen," says Mamá.

"The body of Christ."

"Amen."

The simple, round white wafer now dissolving in her mouth.

"We beg you, O Lord, remember not the sins of her youth, the faults of ignorance, but in your mercy keep her in mind in the brightness of your glory."

"What's going on here?" Antonio asks. "Who's she trying to fool?"

"She's dying," she replies. "She really is dying, Antonio."

The priest takes his leave in silence, and Mamá remains with her eyes closed like a sullied deity.

Joaquín showed up that night, absurdly, buzzing from downstairs, asking to speak to her when she was already in her pajamas and therefore had to get dressed again to go down. Manuel was more surprised than she was, since, deep down, some part of her subconscious had been expecting this visit for weeks. Time had been unnecessarily cruel to Joaquín's face, or at least that was her first thought when she saw him standing there in the doorway, smoking the same brand of cigarettes, wearing the same expression he wore when Mamá called him to the office back when the factory still existed. Looking just as you'd picture an old man described as *tired*—tired hands and eyes, pants either falling down or else belted too high, shirt showing its age by way of coffee-stained cuffs—Joaquín had taken on the humble vulnerability of old age when it still allows a modicum of self-sufficiency. She suggested they go to a nearby bar but he said he'd rather just sit on a bench on the street.

For the first few minutes she got the strange feeling one gets on returning to their childhood home after many years of absence: everything struck her as smaller, more endearing; this man, for whom she'd never felt any particular fondness, now, in his old age, moved her, as though he too had been but another of Mamá's victims.

"How's your mother?"

"She's dying, Joaquín. She's dying." She spoke the words without pity, knowing that Luisa was at the hospital with her and that Mamá might be dying at this very instant, and Joaquín received them, even if he'd already known it deep down, like an unexpected blow and lowered his head.

"I don't know whether I should go see her or not," he said.

"I think it's probably not worth it, Joaquín."

She knew that this was the ultimate punishment, the worst thing she could subject her mother to, and yet the scene with the priest that afternoon, the feeling she'd given Mamá one last opportunity to be sincere, had left her so disillusioned that she now had the fortitude to show no mercy.

"I didn't treat her well."

"No one, in my mother's opinion, has treated her well."

"No, it's not that. . . I mean, I really didn't treat her well."

Suddenly she wanted to console him, to take his hand. Joaquín had abruptly turned serious, solemn, had even stopped looking at her.

"Oh, come now. What was it you did that was so terrible?"

"I burned down the factory."

"What?"

"I burned down the factory."

He'd said it slowly, deliberately, like a regret long-ago shouldered, and she, having been on the verge of consoling him, now felt betrayed, and looked at him with the old mistrust, seeing him as an ungrateful yokel. But then came other feelings. Her initial surprise gave way to a strangely agreeable feeling of compassion; Joaquín was the first person this week to admit he was guilty of something, and this admission not only saved him but, somehow, saved Mamá as well.

"But why?"

"I don't even know anymore," he replied. "I know I did it, and I know that at the time it seemed like the only thing I could do."

Joaquín spoke of his fear with the tender graciousness of an old man describing a childhood passion, as though slightly ashamed yet also fully aware of how important it had been to his life at the time. A part of her had immediately forgiven him, was forgiving him now, as he tried to better explain himself, detailing the days leading up to the fire, describing his fear and regret in the years following as though it were someone else's life, a life absurd yet understandable; another part of her despised him for causing Mamá's unhappiness, and even more than that Antonio's unhappiness, and wanted to slap him then and there.

"But why were you afraid?"

"Five months before the fire I'd asked your mother to marry me. Don't look shocked. We spent all day together, for so long. The truth is I don't even know if I really wanted to marry her, I just knew that I wanted to be with her, to belong to her."

"And how did she respond?"

"She told me she needed a manager, not a husband."

"Mamá," she whispered, and suddenly it was absurd to whisper *Mamá.*

"I wanted to be hers, I suppose, in the same way that the factory was, or you and your brother and sister were; I thought a lot about it, afterward, because if anyone had asked why I was burning the factory down at the time, I wouldn't have known what to say. In the months after I asked her to marry me, I couldn't stand the feeling I had, like I'd been stripped naked. She treated me exactly the same, we'd have lunch and sort out the contractors' paperwork just like always, but I couldn't stand belonging to her then, I felt suffocated. And at the time, your brother had started taking over a lot of things, doing a terrible job, most likely because being her son was too much to live up to."

Joaquín spoke slowly, calmly, as though his words weren't even a confession. She felt her heart racing, and she understood, and understanding saved her.

"What else, Joaquín."

"One night we had to travel to Soria for some machinery repairs, and we spent the night in a hotel. I lost my mind. I told her I loved her. I tried to get into her room. The next day she wouldn't even talk about it. I don't know anymore if I loved her or not, I suppose I probably didn't."

"You didn't love her," she said regretfully.

"I suppose not."

Suddenly it was cold out and the darkness was condensed, as if the night had been cobbled over.

"Do you remember, when I was a little girl, how much I

loved sinking my hands into those big mounds of sawdust?"

"Yes, I remember," Joaquín replied, slightly bewildered by the abrupt change of topic. "You really loved that."

There came a long, absurd silence. Allowing Joaquín to speak to Mamá wouldn't solve anything. Allowing Antonio (who could do nothing else) to put her on trial wouldn't solve anything either. Each sin, through its very commission, contained its own penance; Joaquín's had lasted nearly ten years and now he brought it here, laying it before her, saving her by giving her the chance to be delivered not of her sorrow from that night but her fearfulness since then.

"Do you remember when we used to go to Cádiz in the summer? Do you remember the house we always rented?"

"Of course," Joaquín replied.

She was distancing herself. She was distancing herself now from this man's momentary act of foolishness and from his pain, looking at him with the understandable displeasure of someone contemplating others' weaknesses, or their sexuality; and at the same time feeling the possibility of forgiving him was a magnanimous gesture held out to her on a tray, a one-sided gesture.

"I'll go tomorrow," Joaquín said. "Tomorrow I'll go and tell her everything."

"No."

"Why not?"

She didn't know how to respond, and didn't, not right away. The street was empty, as though awaiting an apparition.

"You won't go because I forgive you."

"Your mother is the one who has to forgive me."

"You don't understand; I forgive you in my mother's name. This is between you and me. Sleep well, Joaquín," she said, standing.

"Thank you."

Walking into her building, she turned and saw him still sitting there on the bench, like a criminal, incredulous that no one was even going to sentence him.

Gone now were resentment, and hatred, and rebellion, and Joaquín, and Alonso Woodworks, and María Fernanda the favorite; now only a woman dying, and dying slowly ("There's no cause for alarm, this initial reaction is simply the effects of the morphine," the doctor had said); like a little girl, she suddenly thought that her mother was like a little girl, and the thought made her smile; Antonio had gone down to the hospital café to have a whisky and it struck her that if they suddenly pulled off the sheets and took off her clothes, Mamá would look like a little girl, and though she now stank of sweat and old-lady smell Mamá still seemed like a little girl. She sat down on the edge of the bed, to more fully submerge herself in this thought, which unexpectedly absolved her mother without requiring almost any effort, like a perfect act of compassion, this happiness accompanied by Mamá's illogical words, "I'm thirsty, give me water," the two of them looking at each other as though, in the end, this alone were enough to understand one another. She'd thought about Joaquín again, thought about him several times that afternoon, imagined his fear, walking into the factory, burning it down, his remorse afterward, when Mamá had refused to have anything to do with him and banished him like a useless guard dog. And if she didn't tell Mamá, it was to avoid the entrance of truth stealing away this woman that Mamá was, perhaps unconsciously, suddenly becoming; "It's so cold in here," but spoken so meekly that she had the urge to bathe her, brush her hair, change her clothes, though only because this woman was so unlike Mamá, only because this new iteration of her performance was so kind, so intimate. She had the urge to cry and it was a pleasant, almost warm feeling, had the urge to hold her hand ("She will probably lose most of her bodily feeling," the doctor had said) and when she did— María Fernanda was probably on the way—she unquestionably felt the proximity of death, like wind on an ice-skater's face she felt Mamá's death blowing in: "It's so cold in here, close the window, María Fernanda."

She could have sworn that not even being confused with María Fernanda upset her. In fact, more than actual confusion it seemed like the last act of Mamá's final performance, a performance that, for the first time, she was enjoying.

"They're already closed."

"No, close them, close them properly."

And she got up, walked to the windows, opened them and them closed them again so that the sounds would accompany her performance, saving her—she thought—from the woman she'd been, with these senseless gestures, this fantasy.

"There."

"I'm still cold."

"No, no, you're fine, you'll see. I'll cover you up and you won't be cold anymore."

"You're the only one who loves me, María Fernanda."

"I know."

And they remained silent for a moment, Mamá quiet, as though recognizing her, and her with the urge to cry, like a woman sentenced to the gallows, waiting for the call which does not come, or at least not in the way she expected, comes instead in the form of sleep, and a coma ("We can keep her alive," the doctor had said, two hours later), and then nothing: Mamá sinking into an empty white sleep, a dream that might or might not feature *her* but would almost certainly feature a bikini-clad twenty-year old María Fernanda bathing in Cádiz, and the factory, and Joaquín or Papá or the outline of any substitutable man. It was as though Mamá were dying in two different times, and less sad than the first death was this other one, eyes closed in a state of peace that was not, in truth, befitting. The very words "keep her alive" were like a retreat within a retreat, and within it the color white, and even further beyond the white was life, absurd, and trivial, and just, and at the same time hard as an almond, but one now shot through with a tiny sliver of comprehension.

"She's dead."

The words "she's dead" on Antonio's lips more real than Mamá's death itself when she called Manuel on the phone, called Maria Fernanda on the phone, absurdly simple how easy the words "she's dead" were to explain that Mamá no longer existed, that she'd gone to sleep after calling her María Fernanda, after saying she was the only one who loved her, Mamá's hands predictable and yet ludicrous, because dead bodies all had some things in common.

They bathed her and dressed her with care, a care both distant and yet familiar, in a blue dress she saved for parties and kept in its dry-cleaning bag at one end of her armoire. Suddenly everything seemed poignant, even the photos of Mamá with Joaquín next to the fan collection at Mamá's house, even María Fernanda arriving at the funeral home with that ridiculous near-histrionic way of sobbing, and Antonio and Luisa silent, and Manuel hugging her, and her wanting to make love to him the moment he walked into the room reserved for Mamá; it was absurd, almost ridiculous, her sudden urge to make love to him, to go home and make slow love, with Mamá there in her coffin, less Mamá than ever, less like in the black-and-white photo of her with Joaquín without ever actually touching Joaquín, or with Papá but without ever touching Papá all the way, or with *them,* her children, but looking as though she were displaying them, holding them up rather than holding them, there with her corkscrew curls, in the photo she'd placed in the living room beside that of Manuel's mother, something about Mamá's thousand faces (or were they all one?) now less Mamá than ever in the coffin.

"What was the last thing she said?" asked María Fernanda, out of nowhere, in the middle of a discussion about making space for Mamá beside Papá in the family plot.

"Last thing she said about what?"

"The last thing Mamá said. Or didn't she say anything?"

She hesitated for a second and was then scandalized at how cleanly she lied, she, who always got so flustered.

"She said, well, first she said she was cold, she kept saying she was cold over and over. She made me close the windows, or, actually, open them and then close them."

"What about us?" asked Antonio, who hadn't said a word up until that moment. "Didn't she say anything about us?"

"She said she loved you."

"Don't lie," Antonio shot back.

"She did, she said she loved you, really, in a very Mamá way of course, in that way Mamá always spoke, but she said she loved you both."

"So how did she say it, then?"

"Can't you see she's trying to tell you? What, you want to interrogate her?" María Fernanda interjected, and the three of them fell silent, hovering on the edge of a lie that, with Mamá dead, now inexplicably united them. "I believe that's what Mamá said. What else would she say?"

"The truth," Antonio replied.

"That was the truth," said María Fernanda.

"No, that was your truth."

Antonio's tone held the simple reproach of a brutish child, and she, who'd never really touched Antonio, who when she kissed him at parties always gave the quick peck of someone trying to void an awkward act of significance, stroked his back with her hand.

"That's what she said, Antonio."

Her death was only real when Manuel pronounced it in bed, and in her children's faces death was real, and in Joaquín's voice on the phone, now distant and understanding, and in the black-and-white photo of Mamá, aged twenty, smiling an elaborate, absurd and out-of-place smile beside Manuel's mother.

ANDRÉS BARBA is one the most lauded contemporary Spanish writers. Winner of the Herralde Prize, he is the author of twelve books, including *Such Small Hands*. His books have been translated into ten languages.

LISA DILLMAN translates from Spanish and Catalan and teaches in the Department of Spanish and Portuguese at Emory University. Some of her recent translations include *Signs Preceding the End of the World*, by Yuri Herrera, which won the 2016 Best Translated Book Award; *Such Small Hands*, by Andrés Barba; *Monastery*, co-translated with Daniel Hahn, by Eduardo Halfon; and *Salting the Wound*, by Víctor del Árbol.

Transit Books is a nonprofit publisher of international and American literature, based in Oakland, California. Founded in 2015, Transit Books is committed to the discovery and promotion of enduring works that carry readers across borders and communities. Visit us online to learn more about our forthcoming titles, events, and opportunities to support our mission.

TRANSITBOOKS.ORG